Delectable Magic

MYRTLEWOOD MYSTERIES BOOK 5

IRIS BEAGLEHOLE

Te Rā Aroha Press

Wellington
New Zealand

Prologue

Detective Constantine Neve yawned as she finished typing up her report on the Summer Festival. It was dark outside the police station and Constable Perkins had gone home hours earlier, leaving her with the bulk of his paperwork.

It was well and truly time for her to be getting home to Nesta, who was keen to celebrate their news about the baby. She experienced a warm and excited sensation when she recalled the phone call they'd received earlier. The baby was fine, healthy, human...and *hers!*

A smile spread across her face just as her phone started to ring again.

She answered it casually, assuming Nesta was calling.

"Detective Neve?" said the rather stiff voice on the other end.

Neve shook herself and responded in a serious tone. "Yes. How can I help you?"

"This is Chief Leopold from the MIB. We've finished our work at the festival site and wanted to inform you of the situation here."

Neve suppressed a sigh. "Yes, Sir. I assume this is too important to wait until morning."

She steeled herself for bad news.

"You're going to want to hear this, Detective."

"How many casualties were there?" Neve asked. The sirens had led so many people into the water, she was dreading the result.

"Actually," said Leopold, his voice becoming less serious and more excited. "There were none. In fact, the opposite."

"What?"

"All the festival attendees are accounted for."

"Amazing," said Neve, beaming. This was turning into a great news day. "Excellent work, Sir."

"Put that down to your witch friends and the vampire volunteers," said Leopold. "We're simply the clean-up crew."

"But what did you mean by the opposite of casualties?" Neve asked with a curious lilt to her voice.

"That's the puzzling thing," he replied. "We've accounted for two extra people."

"*Extra* people?"

"They weren't festival attendees and aren't from around here as far as we know. They shouldn't have been on site."

"That's...well, that's unusual, but surely not a bad thing," said Neve.

"Perhaps not," said Leopold, his voice stilted. "Only...there's something strange about them."

One

Rosemary groaned as she entered Thorn Manor, carrying far too many bags and boxes.

"What is it now?" Athena called from the kitchen. "Are you still grumbling that your vampire suitor hasn't called?"

Rosemary wandered towards her daughter's voice. "No. It's worse than I thought."

She slumped down at the kitchen table and rested her head in her hands. Sure, Burk had been away on business for a week and hadn't so much as sent her a text message, but she had bigger fish to fry.

"What's worse than you thought?"

"The shop...well, it's barely a shop at all at the moment."

"I thought they were supposed to be finished days ago. You said we had plenty of time before the opening."

Rosemary sighed. "Yes, but that's before the main builder got sick and it all had to be pushed out, remember? He said they'd finished the bulk of the work yesterday, but can't do any more this week. So I went have a look this morning. And…"

"That bad?" said Athena.

"Worse than I thought. I suppose the actual building work has mostly been done."

"So what's the problem?" Athena asked.

"The whole place is a mess. It's all covered in sawdust and regular dust, and other kinds of dust. Some of the edging isn't finished. It looks like a tip. We're supposed to be opening up the day after tomorrow. Maybe we'll have to delay."

"But we already sent out all those invitations," said Athena, frowning as she carried a tray of tea to the table. She opened a small bottle of Marjie's special remedy and added a double dose to her mother's cup before serving the tea.

"Thanks," said Rosemary, taking a sip. "I needed that."

After a few more sips she began to feel herself perking up a little. "I suppose we don't really need to have a grand opening party."

"Oh, don't be silly," said Athena. "You and Marjie have already put so much work into it. Hey, I'll text her."

"Oh, no, don't bother Marjie. She's already done enough."

"Do you think she'd forgive me if I didn't tell her what was going on?" Athena asked sharply.

Rosemary's shoulders sank. "Fair point." She gulped down the rest of her tea.

Athena's text message got an almost instant reply. "She'll be over in a jiffy."

Rosemary let out a long slow breath. "She is such a gem, isn't she? What on earth would we do without Marjie?"

"I don't even want to think about it," said Athena.

Scarcely ten minutes passed before Marjie bowled into Thorn Manor, barely knocking on the door. "It's all going to be fine," she insisted.

"How can you say that?" said Rosemary. "Did you see the place? It's a right mess. I mean, I hate to cancel after all the work we've put into planning the party but—"

"Nonsense," said Marjie. "I've had a look at the shop. All it needs is a bit of a scrub and a few bits and pieces to be fixed. We've got all the skills we need around town. And I've already started calling people in. We're going to have a working bee."

"Are you serious?" said Rosemary.

"Of course I'm serious." Margie scowled. "Stop your sulking. We've got a lot of work to do."

Rosemary wasn't sure if it was Marjie's special formula or just the way that she told her off in such a loving and almost comical manner, but she perked right up. "All right. No more sulking," she vowed.

Athena shot her a skeptical look.

"At least not for a little while," Rosemary added. "We've got a working bee to attend to."

The following morning passed in a cacophony of activity around the shop.

After several hours, Rosemary popped outside for a quick breather. Liam, Nesta, Una, and Ashwyn were all inside cleaning down the surfaces with some delightful smelling oils and finishing off the last of the edgings that the builders hadn't had time to fix. Meanwhile, Ferg balanced on a ladder, hanging the new striped mint green-and-lavender awning.

Rosemary leaned against a lamp post. She was tired after spending a good few hours cleaning the floors.

"All done with the surfaces," said Liam, walking towards Rosemary.

"Thanks so much for all your help," said Rosemary. "You're a lifesaver. The builders weren't going to make it back here until next week. I thought about cancelling the opening, but Marjie wouldn't have any of it."

Liam chuckled. "Anytime. You know I'm always happy to help."

"You're a good friend," said Rosemary.

Liam raised an eyebrow about that.

"What?" Rosemary asked.

"Well, look, I know you've been on a few dates with Perseus."

Rosemary nodded. "Yes. Except that I tend to call him Burk, which is probably a little impersonal, but it suits him." She bit her tongue to stop herself from rambling. This conversation with Liam was starting to feel a little awkward.

"I know," he said. "And look, I respect that. But I won't be able to forgive myself if I don't..."

"Don't what?"

"Rosey, do you remember when you first came back to town?" Liam asked, his blue-green eyes glinting in the sun as the breeze ruffled his sandy hair.

Rosemary didn't know what to say. When she'd first arrived back in town and had bumped into Liam again it certainly had brought back a wave of nostalgia for the fleeting romance they'd had as teenagers. Not long afterwards, he'd asked her on a date, which she'd had to refuse seeing as she wasn't dating at that time. All that was before she knew he was a werewolf. They'd spent a fair bit of time together since, especially since Rosemary had helped him keep his wolfie problem under control using magic. "What is it, Liam?" she asked, feeling her discomfort increasing.

"I was thinking about it the other day...and you said that when you did start dating, I would be the first one you'd call, or something like that. I can't remember the exact words you used. And I'm not going to hold you to something that you said in passing."

Rosemary shook her head. "Seriously?"

"Look, Rosey. The thing is, before things get serious with Burk, I just wondered if you'd give me a chance."

Rosemary meant to say no instantly, but then she hesitated. Burk had been so distant recently and she'd been feeling rather lonely. Apparently thousand-year-old vampires weren't much into texting and making phone calls to keep in touch. She wondered what kind of relationship they even had from time to time. They hadn't made any kind of commitment and had only been on one official date. All this probably played a part in her next words.

"Okay, Liam."

"What?" His jaw dropped.

"Look, Burk and I have been on a few dates. We've had a nice time. We're not exactly intimate. I mean, not that you need to know that. And I'm rambling again. But anyway, I haven't seen him in a while. We've never made any promises to each other."

"So you'll go out with me?" A grin spread across his face.

"I suppose we could have one date and see how it goes. But I guess I'll have to tell Burk about it. Otherwise, it would be very dishonest or dishonorable or something like that. Also, I don't have a lot of time at the moment, so you'll have to fit around the shop hours, plus I'm bound to be exhausted in the evenings for the next little while."

Liam continued to grin. "I didn't think that was going to work."

"What do you mean?" Rosemary frowned. "I'm a reasonable person. And I do recall saying that I would go out with you when I started dating. But I just don't really know how to do this dating thing. And I don't really know if I should be in a relationship at all."

Liam held up a finger to quiet her. "Just let me enjoy this," he said, continuing to grin. "I want to enjoy the moment. And don't worry. It's okay. You're not promising anything. I just wanted to have a chance to spend some time with you."

"We could do that as friends, you know," Rosemary muttered.

"Friends, or something more." Liam gave a carefree shrug and, with that, he left.

Rosemary watched her werewolf friend walk off down the street with a spring in his step and was hit by a sudden sense of dread. What had she gotten herself into?

Two

"Over here!" Elise called with a laugh. She darted across one of the many wooden rope bridges that led from the little house in the trees where she lived with her mother, and grandfather and grandmother, pulling Athena behind her.

"Where are we going?" Athena asked, looking around at the dark forest all around them.

"You'll see," said Elise. "Come on."

She led the way, climbing up a wooden ladder between two trees going up quite high.

Athena felt slightly disorientated.

"Don't worry, it's safe," said Elise. "Just hold on tight and don't look down."

She laughed again and Athena joined in.

Elise's laughter was always infectious.

It was close to midnight. Elise and Athena had enjoyed a nice late dinner with Elise's family. They'd spent the evening chatting in her loft room for several hours before Elise had suddenly decided a late night adventure was in order.

"I haven't taken anyone up here before," said Elise.

"I feel special, then."

"Here." Elise had reached the top of the ladder and held out her hand to help Athena up.

"What is this?" said Athena as her legs adjusted to unstable footing. "Some kind of net?"

"Exactly," said Elise.

Athena took a closer look to find that a net that looked to be made of strong ropes was strung between the trees.

Elise laughed and pulled Athena towards her. They both tumbled down.

Athena shrieked momentarily before the net caught them. She lay in Elise's arms.

"You scared me!" Athena grumbled playfully.

"So?" said Elise. They're both giggled for a few moments.

"This is cool," Athena said. "Is it a nymph thing, you know, to put nets up in the air like this?"

"I suppose so," said Elise. "Some of the other forest dwellers do it too. But this one has the best view."

Athena looked around before Elise gestured upwards. They both sighed looking at the shining constellations of stars and the half-moon hanging low in the sky. It was a stunning view between the trees, as the forest canopy opened up.

"There not many lights out here, I suppose," said Athena. "The stars are so bright."

"It's how we like it," said Elise, holding Athena closer and kissing her cheek.

"It's so nice just to be here." Athena leaned into Elise's embrace. "Like I don't have a care in the world. At least we don't have to worry about school for a while since it's the summer holidays. And nothing terrible has happened recently."

"Touch wood," said Elise.

Athena reached out and tapped on the tree branch nearest her.

"I'm sorry I can't make the chocolate shop opening," Elise said.

"It's totally fine," said Athena. "Your cousin's wedding takes precedence."

"I'm also sorry I was so silly."

"What do you mean? I like that you're silly." Athena could hardly see in the low light emitted from the stars and moon, but she was willing to bet that Elise's blue hair was tinging pink. She sounded slightly embarrassed.

Athena reached forward and kissed her softly. After a moment she pulled away. "Right, now tell me what it is that's bothering you."

"I just feel so silly about getting jealous of you and Finnigan. I know you don't like him like that anymore. I just...maybe I'm a jealous person. Insecure..."

Athena shook her head. "Don't worry about it. It's fine."

Elise sighed. "I have been thinking about it a lot," she admitted.

"You're still worried about Finnigan?"

"I don't know," said Elise. "It's not just him. I'm worried about losing you."

"Why do you think that is?" Athena asked. "It's not like I'm planning on going anywhere."

Elise shrugged. "That's what I've been wondering. It's probably to do with my dad. You know, he just left when he figured out that there was something strange about us. He was human and we were magical...and he just left. He abandoned me."

Elise's voice choked up a little. A tear gleamed in the darkness on her cheek. Athena reached up and brushed it away. "It's not your fault. Just because your dad was weak and ridiculous. It doesn't mean anything about you at all."

"It doesn't feel like that though," said Elise. "Ever since I was younger...ever since he left, I always felt like there should have been something I could have done. If I'd been better...I know it's probably ridiculous and irrational and all, but that's how it feels. It's personal."

"I get that," said Athena. "But honestly, it's you I..."

"I know," said Elise, shrugging. "But I can't really get you to promise never to leave me, can I?"

Athena laughed. "Sounds a bit intense considering we've only been together for a month or two."

Elise sighed. "Maybe I am a bit intense."

"I like how intense you are," said Athena, cuddling her girl-friend. "And you have nothing to be insecure about. You're a wonderful, intelligent, gorgeous person and I love you." It was the first time she'd said anything quite like that to anyone, romantically.

Athena's heart pounded in her chest and she panicked. Had she overstepped some boundary? Was it too soon?

Elise stared at her, then she smiled and buried her face in Athena's neck. "I love you too."

They lay there, suspended in the trees, staring at the stars, and Athena realised she'd never quite felt so happy in all of her life... but with that knowledge came a creeping concern. Something was bound to come and take all this happiness away.

Three

Rosemary sighed happily, inhaling the warm and fragrant late summer air. She stepped up onto a ladder to put up the small wooden hanging sign, artfully painted to read Myrtlewood Chocolates. She smiled as gentle Bach cello music drifted out from the shop.

The frantic rush of the last two days had eased and excitement replaced her previous stress. As the sign clicked into place, something inside her seemed to do the same. This was her dream...her big, long-term dream. It was all becoming reality. She watched through the window as Athena and Marjie arranged things behind the counter.

Rosemary had returned from the Summer Solstice festival, delighted to see the progress on the renovations. All the work had been completed to the exact specifications she'd wanted. They had painted the walls a calming sage green and made the most of the natural wood already inside of the shop, polishing up the panelling and converting the old bar into a shiny new-looking counter. The booths had been restored in a calming lavender velvet, so that customers could sit and enjoy their hot chocolates, and the old threadbare striped awning outside had been replaced with a brand new one. The stripes were now lavender and green to match the interior.

She got down from the ladder and took a step back to take it all in.

Everything looked gorgeous.

"Just as you imagined it, dear?" Marjie asked, poking her head out of the front door, clearly responding to Rosemary's satisfied expression.

"Everything I dreamed and more." Rosemary beamed.

"It's great and all," said Athena, coming out to appraise the shop from the outside, "but shouldn't we do something for the grand opening? Maybe wrap it all up in a giant ribbon that you can cut?"

Rosemary laughed nervously. "I don't think so. Giant novelty ribbons remind me of estate agents, and you know I'm allergic."

Athena laughed. "I can't believe you're still deluded about that," she said, coming over to put an arm around her mother's shoulder. "But we still love you, anyway."

"Oh, thanks love. How sweet of you."

"Sweet as chocolate!" said a warm booming voice from behind them.

Rosemary turned, delighted to see Papa Jack, the good friend she had made on her chocolatier course. He was dressed in a white shirt with black pants, suspenders, and a purple bow tie. A little girl of about seven clung to his arm with long light brown hair, golden skin, and dark eyes.

"You made it!" Rosemary exclaimed. "And this must be little Zoya." Rosemary smiled at the girl.

"Of course I made it!" he crowed, giving Rosemary a big hug.

Rosemary introduced Athena and Marjie. There were smiles all-round, though it was hard not to feel happiness in Papa Jack's warm presence.

"You came all the way from London just for the opening?" Marjie asked as little Zoya peeked tentatively through the door of the shop.

"Go ahead, take a look inside," said Athena encouragingly. Zoya beamed at her, then skipped into the shop.

"Wouldn't miss the grand opening for the world!" said Papa Jack. He gestured to Rosemary. "This one was the saving grace of my study experience. Besides, I'd like to take you up on the job offer, if it's still standing."

"Of course!" said Rosemary. "I'd be a fool to turn down an application from someone with all your years of experience in business – plus you're an excellent chocolatier, and didn't you say you've been a magic-user, yourself?"

"I've dabbled," said Papa Jack modestly.

Zoya came running back out of the shop and leapt into her grandfather's arms. "It's so pretty inside!" she exclaimed. "Come and look."

Rosemary gave a brief tour of the new shop, which was received with much admiration from Papa Jack, particularly the special chocolatier kitchen.

He rubbed his hands together in glee. "It's more beautiful than I imagined. I can't wait to get started."

Rosemary smiled. "It's funny," she said, looking towards Athena. "My favourite 90s grunge music is playing now, whereas before it was my favourite Bach cello suite. Did you set up a playlist with all the best songs for me?"

Athena scrunched up her nose. "What are you talking about? They're playing something more modern and intense than any of that."

Rosemary looked around, baffled. "Where's the stereo system?"

Marjie just laughed. "Oh, you two!"

"What?" Rosemary asked.

Marjie grinned. "I thought you knew about the field."

"Field?" Athena asked.

"Covvey had it installed back when this place was a dodgy old bar. It plays whatever music people want to hear. I'm surprised it's still going strong after all this time."

Rosemary and Athena laughed in surprise.

"Well, all I can hear is some quiet jazz," Papa Jack said, with a shrug. "It's pleasant."

"Brilliant!" said Athena. "I won't have to be subjected to Mum's terrible taste in music."

Marjie nodded sagely. "I do believe that's exactly why Covvey had it installed, dear. He didn't want to be subject to anyone else's musical preferences. As I recall, he preferred silence, himself. Besides, he was sick of his patrons starting fights over the old jukebox."

"Magic is just so wonderful!" Papa Jack crowed, lifting Zoya up in his arms and spinning her around gently.

Rosemary, Athena, and Marjie beamed at each other. Papa Jack's enthusiasm was contagious.

"The opening's not for a few hours," said Marjie. "So there's plenty of time for morning tea first. Why don't you all come over to my shop for refreshments? Have a little break before we all get stuck in."

Rosemary hesitated, feeling she already had so much to do, but Marjie was persistent, and tempted her with an offer of a lamb pastie, straight from the oven.

They walked the three shops down, past Liam's bookshop, and enjoyed morning tea at Marjie's. Zoya seemed to be in heaven with a large slice of chocolate cake, and Papa Jack exclaimed delightedly the whole time about Marjie's shop, and other features he'd noticed around the town. He even managed to quickly strike up a friendship with Marjie's quiet and sullen husband, Herb, over a mutual love of trains.

"What a lovely gentleman," Marjie remarked as she cleared the table, watching the two men chat over the counter. "I don't think I've seen Herb have such a long conversation. Not for years!"

Rosemary smiled. "Yes. He's a good sort."

Marjie and Athena accompanied Papa Jack and Zoya back into the shop while Rosemary ran a few last-minute errands, including picking up some supplies for the opening party.

By the time she returned she was surprised at the transformation.

"Marjie, your decorating skills are without compare," Rosemary said as she took in all the balloons and streamers that hung from the ceiling, matching the purple and green tones of the shop.

"Oh, it's nothing, dear," said Marjie. "Little Zoya here helped instruct me on where best to put things."

It wasn't long before people started arriving for the opening, which drew quite a good turnout from the town.

Covvey and Agatha had arrived early, and Rosemary offered them some chocolate drops from a wicker basket. Agatha took quite a few pieces, some of which she stashed in her handbag, refusing a serviette when Rosemary offered it to her, with a slightly guilty smile that reminded Rosemary of a young child with their hand in the cookie jar.

Covvey was rather gruff, as usual. "I'm just here to see what you've done with the place."

He carefully examined the interior of the shop.

Rosemary waited, not wanting to anger her wolf shifter landlord. After a few moments of Covvey running his hands along the old wooden panelling and checking out the kitchen, he returned and nodded curtly.

"It's alright, I suppose," he said and stormed off.

"What's with that man?" Athena asked. "You think he'd be happy we're looking after the place."

"Oh, don't mind the grumpy old codger," said Agatha. "He seems satisfied enough. He won't give you any trouble."

Rosemary was slightly relieved to hear this. She handed Agatha a chocolate goodie bag to take away before she left.

Neve and Nesta arrived, smiling warmly.

"The baby's growing fast," said Rosemary, smiling at Nesta, who was glowing.

"We can't stay long, I'm afraid," said Nesta. "We've got a midwife appointment."

Neve looked worried for a moment but quickly reinstated her smile.

"Not even for a quick hot chocolate?" Rosemary asked.

"Maybe a little one. We just thought we'd stop in and give you this." Nesta handed them an envelope.

It was cream with a subtle silver floral pattern. Rosemary opened it, delighted to find a wedding invitation.

"How wonderful!" said Athena. "Congratulations!"

"We'll definitely be there," said Rosemary, taking her turn for a hug.

"You'd better be," said Nesta. "It wouldn't be the same without you."

Rosemary retrieved a couple of small hot chocolates for Neve and Nesta, taking care to ensure the calming one went to Neve. As she handed them their drinks, she gently pulled Neve aside.

"What's going on? Are you still worried about the baby?"

Neve laughed nervously. "The baby, the wedding...oh, and did I tell you some extra people were found after the Summer Solstice festival?"

Rosemary shook her head. "What do you mean?"

"I'm really not sure, but I got a call a few days ago from the MIB cleanup lead. It's brilliant that they managed to account for all the festival attendees, but there were two extra people found on that beach and they were...odd."

"Odd how?" Rosemary felt an icy chill in her gut.

Neve took a sip of her drink and visibly relaxed. "Apparently they were glowing at first, and seemed to be in a trance. They didn't talk or anything. After a while, the glowing faded and they fell into some kind of coma."

"Where are they?" Rosemary asked, curious.

"Up in Sláintebail."

"Huh?"

"You know," said Neve. "The magical hospital. And before you ask, no you won't be able to go and sleuth on them there. The hospital has very tight security."

"Hey, I didn't say anything," Rosemary protested.

Neve crossed her arms. "I know that look in your eyes, Rosemary. You're suspicious."

Rosemary bit her lower lip. "What if they're some kind of spies sent by the sirens or the Bloodstone Society?"

Neve rolled her eyes. "Don't start that. They're locked up in hospital. They aren't spying on anyone."

"Maybe not yet," said Rosemary suspiciously. "Or you think they could be doing some kind of magic while in a coma?"

Neve shook her head. "If anything, the magic was probably done to them. I don't know why you think the poor patients are dodgy."

Rosemary shrugged. "I'm just on guard for anything that might cause us more danger and mayhem."

Neve gave Rosemary a hug. "Everything is fine. You're doing great. Congratulations on the shop."

"Thanks," said Rosemary. "Congratulations on the engagement!"

The opening party continued for several hours longer than Rosemary had anticipated due to the large volume of people arriving. In fact, there were far too many people to fit inside the little shop itself. They sprawled out onto the sidewalk.

Papa Jack was quick to don one of Rosemary's sage green-and-purple aprons and pitch in to help. He and Marjie made a formidable team, serving up hot chocolate mixtures that Rosemary had prepared earlier.

As they finally began to close up in the early evening, a rather unwelcome visitor appeared out of thin air.

Rosemary recognised Reginald immediately, mostly from his familiar top hat.

"Not you again," Rosemary grumbled.

The man stuttered, clearly used to far more admiration.

"I told you I'm not interested," Rosemary continued.

"Ms Thorn, you would do well to respect the Arch Magistrate and the powers of the witching parliament in Bermuda that I am bestowed with."

There was a hush around the room as the remaining customers listened.

Reginald cleared his throat and continued. "You may not like me personally, but I assure you..."

"Oh no," said Rosemary. "This is nothing personal – well, not about you anyway. I just don't have any particular knowledge or interest or regard for Bermuda, and I don't want to go there. In fact, I don't want anything to do with any matter that concerns the Bracewell-Thorns."

"I assure you this is not at all about your cousins, or your aunt and uncle for that matter. The matter at hand is much more serious and pressing."

"Oh yes," said Rosemary, rolling her eyes. "I have to say I'm feeling rather tired of all the serious pressing urgent, dangerous situations. Still not interested."

"What is it about?" Athena asked.

"I cannot reveal the details," said Reginald. "Matters concerning the witching parliament are of the utmost secrecy, but I can assure you they are very important and you must attend."

"You lost me at secrecy," said Rosemary. "We've had quite enough of that."

Four

That evening, they sat around a large table at The Witches' Wort, recovering from the busy day. Zoya helped the foundling twins choose food from the kids menu. Una and Ashwyn smiled as they watched the children all getting along so well.

"This place is amazing!" said Papa Jack, looking around at the warm and rustic interior of the pub.

Rosemary smiled. "Well, I'm glad we brought you here. Besides, I was definitely too tired to cook."

"I'm talking about the whole thing," said Papa Jack. "This place, Myrtlewood. A whole magical town!"

"It's takes some getting used to," said Athena.

"No, deary," he replied. "I'm right at home. It feels like I've been waiting for this place my entire life."

"Well, we're glad you're here," said Marjie warmly. "Any friend of Rosemary's is already part of the family."

"Here, here!" said Ferg, lifting his glass. He'd showed up towards the end of the opening party and had stayed to help clean up, insisting it was an important part of being a responsible citizen.

"You know," said Athena. "I think we should take that little man up on his offer."

"What are you talking about, dear?" Marjie asked.

"That man from Bermuda," Athena explained.

"*You* want to go to the witching parliament?" Rosemary asked, surprised. "I didn't know teens could be so interested in bureaucracy."

Athena laughed. "I bet it's all very interesting and grand. But I must admit, what I'm really wanting is a trip to a tropical island. I've never been abroad and it sounds like a great excuse for a holiday."

She held up her phone, peppered with images of Bermuda resorts.

"I bet it's not at all like that!" said Rosemary.

"Oh, I hear it is," said Marjie. "At least a little."

"What have you heard?" Rosemary asked. She was curious to know more about Bermuda, even though she was determined never to go there.

"Oh, you know, bits and pieces. The parliamentary side of things is very formal, I hear, but the rest of it is a different kind of splendour. The fancy witching folk go there for holidays and to feel self-important," said Marjie with a chuckle. "I hear they live it up in luxury over there."

"See, Mum, just what we need," said Athena. "Come on. My birthday's coming up and a trip overseas would be a great way to celebrate."

"Ooh!" said Marjie. "A seventeenth birthday! How exciting! That's the age of magical maturation. You'll be considered a proper adult."

Athena grinned smugly in Rosemary's direction.

"Maybe by the witching world," said Rosemary. "But I'm still your legal guardian for a whole other year."

Athena frowned and then turned on the puppy dog eyes and stared imploringly.

"Athena," said Rosemary. "You wanted a party here, remember? Besides, we can afford to take our own proper holidays now. How about once we're settled at the shop we plan a nice getaway?"

"Maybe," said Athena, slumping over her phone again.

Sherry arrived at the table to take their orders. Rosemary watched as the pub owner listened closely to Ferg's overly complex dietary demands. Sherry looked to be healthy, though she was still a little aloof. She had kept her distance, as if deliberately avoiding Rosemary since the incident a few months earlier where she'd stolen an important Thorn family heirloom. The emerald pendant, in fact, that Rosemary always wore around her neck because it helped to magically centre her, making her less scattered and erratic.

Rosemary still considered Sherry a friend, and had long forgiven her for the incident, especially as her motive had involved rescuing a missing girl, but things hadn't quite been the same since between them.

Sherry reached Rosemary last to take her order.

"What will it be, then?"

Rosemary smiled. "Sherry," she said. "It's good to see you."

"Oh," said Sherry, blushing a little. "Thank you, Rosemary."

Rosemary lowered her voice. "You don't have to keep your distance. Water under the bridge..."

"I appreciate that," said Sherry quietly. "It's just...oh, you know. Shame, I guess."

"What you did turned out to be incredibly noble and heroic," Rosemary said. "Like I've told you before."

"It's not just that," said Sherry. "Things have been odd, lately. I haven't been very social. Just keeping to myself."

"Anything you need help with?" Rosemary asked.

"I wouldn't want to trouble you," said Sherry. "But if you must know, I keep getting this feeling...a kind of prickling on the back of my neck, like something's wrong."

"Do you think it could be the fae realm?" Athena asked, losing interest in her phone and joining the conversation again. "You were so sensitive to it around the equinox."

Sherry shrugged. "It's probably nothing. Pay it no mind. Now, Rosemary, what do you want for dinner?"

Just as Rosemary finished placing her order of the beef, thyme, and mushroom pie, music started up from the other side of the pub.

"Who's that?" Athena asked, staring.

Rosemary looked over to see a young man, probably in his mid-twenties, with an acoustic guitar decorated as if it were covered in leaves. He wore a green waistcoat over an old-fashioned white shirt, and worn jeans. His brown hair was long enough to flop over his face and he was clearly very handsome.

"A travelling minstrel!" said Sherry excitedly. "Isn't he wonderful?"

Rosemary was slightly surprised by Sherry's change in demeanour. "He's certainly talented with the guitar," she admitted, watching his fingers dance deftly across the strings, producing a delightful tune. Then the man began to sing in a deep, soft, sweet, and lilting voice. "And a great singer."

The rest of the pub had fallen silent as they listened, as if awestruck. Rosemary recognised the lyrics of the old folk ballad 'John Barley Corn'. The first verse, he sang slowly, but as he reached the chorus, the music quickened and people got up to dance.

Rosemary followed suit as everyone in the pub suddenly felt the joyful urge to move to the beat of the music. Tables were moved to the side to clear a dance floor and wild impromptu folk dancing followed.

Burk appeared through the crowd, and Rosemary was immediately drawn to the handsome vampire. He took her hand and spun her around.

Rosemary had a moment of worrying if they were all enchanted, as it really was such fun. Then she reminded herself that when she'd been spell-bound by sirens she hadn't had the sense to question it. Reassured, she continued dancing for several songs until the minstrel took a break and they returned to their table to find dinner waiting.

"Join us," Rosemary said to Burk.

"Thank you, I'll take you up on the offer." He smiled, grabbing a chair from one of the surrounding empty tables and sitting down next to Rosemary. "I'm sorry I couldn't be at your opening."

"That's okay," said Rosemary, lowering her voice. "Too much sun risk?"

Burk nodded, looking around the table.

"I should have thought of that and held it a little later."

"Don't be ridiculous," said Burk. "It's a daytime shop. It makes no sense to have the opening party at night just for me. Besides, the days are still so long at this time of year. I'm used to hibernating a little. Now tell me, who are your new friends?"

"Oh, where are my manners?" said Rosemary, before introducing Burk to Papa Jack and Zoya.

"Lovely to meet you," said Papa Jack. "That was brilliant! Such fun with the dancing! Is it always like this here?"

"It's always...different," said Rosemary. "I haven't seen that man play before or done any dancing in the pub, but it seems to be the thing to do whenever a minstrel is in town."

"Isn't he wonderful?" said Athena, looking all doe eyed towards the musician who now stood at the bar. "Hey, do you think he can play at my birthday party?"

"You could ask," said Rosemary. "But as he's a *travelling* minstrel, and your birthday is not for a few weeks, who knows if he'll still be around."

"I'm too shy!" Athena cried, and Rosemary eyed her suspiciously.

"Don't tell me you have a little crush on the musician."

Athena blushed. "Shut up, Mum!"

"I'll ask for you," said Burk. "Which day?"

"Thank you," Athena said. "Saturday the seventh of August. We're having the party here at the pub."

He got up and strode over to the bar, returning moments later. "I've booked you a travelling minstrel," he said to Athena.

She beamed at him and then glared at her mother.

"August," said Papa Jack, smiling. "A little Leo."

"Yes," said Athena. "But I'm a bit quiet for a Leo. I have Virgo rising, and a Gemini Moon." She was always pleased to show off her astrological knowledge – it had become her favourite subject at school.

"Ah, that explains it," said Papa Jack. "A tricky combination."

"Tricky indeed," said Rosemary.

Athena stuck out her tongue at her mother. "Burk, since you're here, maybe you can help me convince my mother that a trip overseas would be a great birthday treat."

"Anywhere but Bermuda," said Rosemary.

"Bermuda?" Burk asked with a strange expression on his face.

"Yes," said Athena. "But let's talk about this later. The music is starting up again. Time to dance!"

The minstrel had started playing a jaunty jig. He was singing about the sun god, Lugh. They all got up from the table, but before Rosemary could move very far, Burk reached out to gently grasp her forearm.

"Rosemary," he said.

"What is it?" she asked.

"I just wanted to inquire as to whether..."

"Is something wrong?"

"No," said Burk. "Quite the opposite. I'm just trying to find the right words to ask you out on another date."

Rosemary beamed at him. "Save your words. Of course I'll accept."

"Excellent," said Burk.

"Err..." Rosemary felt a wave of panic. She needed to tell Burk about Liam, but she didn't know how to. In her typical style, she blurted it all out before restraining herself. "So...you see. I'm going to go on one date with him, but it doesn't mean anything in particular."

"I see," said Burk, looking slightly taken aback.

"Sorry!" said Rosemary. "I wasn't really sure where we stand, and I hadn't heard from you in a while..."

"You don't have anything to apologise for," said Burk. "How's next Wednesday?"

"What?"

"For our date?"

"Perfect," said Rosemary, sighing in relief. She allowed Burk to take her arm and lead her to the dance floor while she marvelled at somehow avoiding a rom-com style drama, despite the situation.

It was a little later than Rosemary had anticipated by the time she and Athena arrived back at Thorn manor.

"Straight to bed," said Rosemary.

"You don't have to tell me, I'm exhausted!" Athena replied.

"Wait a minute," said Rosemary, looking at her phone.

"What?" Athena asked.

"A voice message, probably nothing urgent."

"You don't think you should check, just in case?" Athena asked. "It might be something important to do with the shop."

"Oh fine," said Rosemary.

She checked the message and immediately groaned.

"Rosemary? Hello?"

"Oh I suppose she's not there."

"Leave a message then!"

"Hello, Rosemary. It's your father calling."

"Parents!"

"Your parents calling. Your mother's here too."

"We just wanted to let you know that since we've finished up our last mission and are back in Stratton, we thought we'd pay you a visit."

"Oh no..." said Rosemary.

"What is it?" Athena asked.

"Brace yourself for an onslaught of preaching. Your grandparents are coming to visit."

Athena laughed. "I bet Bermuda doesn't sound so bad now!"

Five

Athena rolled over in bed and stared at the ceiling. She was feeling distinctly uncomfortable. Her whole body felt as though it was tingling.

It wasn't unpleasant, but it was unwelcome. The last thing she needed was more oddness, just when things had started to settle down.

Her phone beeped.

It was a message from Elise.

Are you up?

Athena replied. *Yes, let's talk.*

Athena was feeling exhausted, but she also felt like she should talk to somebody about whatever was going on with her body.

Besides, she'd been missing Elise.

"How was your cousin's wedding?" she asked when Elise called.

"Oh, you know, just the usual rainbow nymph family traditions. It was great."

"Cool," said Athena. "I wish I could have seen it."

"There'll be photos. How was the chocolate shop opening?"

"Surprisingly good. There were no dramas, and then we went to the pub and there was dancing."

"Fabulous. It sounds like you had a wonderful time."

Athena sighed. "I did."

"So then why do you sound slightly anxious?"

"I just feel really strange."

"Strange how?"

"All tingly. I don't know...a bit like I'm not really myself."

"I don't like the sound of that. I'll be back soon and I can help you figure out what's going on. Are you going to tell your mum?"

"I don't know," said Athena. "It might all be over in the morning. I'm tired."

"I should sleep too. I'm so exhausted."

"I miss you," said Athena. "It feels like ages since you've been gone."

"A few days."

"Yeah." Athena leaned into the phone, as if warming herself with the sound of Elise's voice.

"It does feel like a long time to be away from you," said Elise. "It just makes me realize how much I love you. Oops! I didn't mean to say that over the phone."

Athena smiled and then laughed.

"I'm sorry," Elise said awkwardly.

"Don't be sorry," said Athena. Some moments later, she quietly added, "I love you too."

She lay there, still on the phone, basking in a beautiful feeling that she knew was nothing to do with magic but felt mystical all the same.

"I can't wait to see you again," said Elise finally.

They ended the call. Athena put her own phone away on the dresser and then collapsed back into her bed. She knew her feelings for Elise were real. But the other thing she was feeling...well... she thought back to the evening earlier.

Things had been rather odd.

The man has appeared with his guitar and his beautiful voice and she'd felt attracted to him. Her mother's teasing had been uncalled for, but she was right.

Athena had experienced some kind of strange momentary infatuation for the man she didn't know at all.

"Maybe it's just exhaustion," she mumbled to herself. "My brain playing tricks on me...Maybe I ate something weird. Mum's funny chocolates. Either way, this has been quite disconcerting."

Whatever happened, she hoped she'd never lose control of her body again.

R osemary answered the door to find Liam standing on the steps.

It was fairly early in the morning and fortunately Athena was still fast asleep. What she didn't know would lead to less heckling for Rosemary.

She and Liam had made arrangements to go for a walk.

Since Rosemary was going to be busy throughout the days and exhausted in the evenings for the next little while getting the shop up and running, they'd decided on an early morning rendezvous. It also suited Rosemary that going for a morning stroll was one of the least romantic dates she could think of, except that Liam had come prepared for something a little more interesting.

"What's all this?" Rosemary asked, gesturing to the wicker basket Liam was holding. "I thought we were just going for a walk before breakfast."

Liam winked. "And I have breakfast here for after the walk."

Rosemary laughed. "You're incorrigible. Here I am dressed in my exercise clothing, not my picnic clothing at all."

"Rosey, I know you better than to believe that you would have separate clothing for picnics."

Rosemary shrugged. "You're right. I don't even have exercise clothing."

She was wearing jeans with a dark green top and a purple woollen jumper. Liam was dressed in a short sleeved shirt and she wondered if werewolves didn't feel the cold, though as it was still summer, it was bound to warm up soon.

"Ready?" he said, offering his arm.

"Okay then," said Rosemary. She locked her hand through Liam's arm but kept a safe distance as they began their walk.

"It must be nice to be out with someone in the daytime," said Liam.

Rosemary gave him a push. "I thought you wanted to spend time with me, not talk about vampires."

"I do indeed want to spend time with you. What would you like to talk about?"

"To be honest, my brain is fried," Rosemary admitted. "But it is nice to be getting out and about in a relaxed way. The shop has been taking up so much of my brain power and energy that I've hardly thought about anything else."

"Well, we don't even have to talk at all," said Liam. "Unless you want to. I'm all for comfortable silences."

They meandered for a while, Liam leading the way towards a small park surrounded by an apple orchard.

"This is nice," said Rosemary. "I didn't even know this was here."

"I know the best kept secrets of this place," Liam said with a cheeky grin. "I've been here a long time. Though not as long as some people. I am only forty, after all."

"Stop that," said Rosemary. "This isn't a competition."

Liam sighed and smiled at her. "No, it's not a competition. I actually felt kind of guilty for putting you on the spot the other day. You don't owe me anything, Rosemary. I owe you a huge debt of gratitude. Your magic has helped me so much. In the last month or two I've really been able to turn my life around. I've stopped skulking in the bookshop all the time. I started smiling more."

"I've noticed that," said Rosemary. "It's nice."

"And how do I repay you?" said Liam with a chuckle. "By pressuring you go on a date with me."

Rosemary shrugged. "You weren't really pressuring me. And maybe I should be exploring my options. I don't know. All this romantic stuff is just really foreign to me. I'm not a natural dater."

"Neither am I," said Liam. "I can't remember the last time I went out with anyone. I avoided it for years because of my... condition. But I do like spending time with friends in the park." He spread out a tartan picnic blanket and began unloading croissants, cheese, ham, scones, clotted cream, and jam from the picnic basket.

"This is quite a spread," said Rosemary. "Very thoughtful."

Liam grinned at her. "I'm a thoughtful kind of guy."

Rosemary bit into a croissant and frowned.

"What is it?" Liam asked.

"I feel kind of guilty," she admitted. "You know I was spending time with Burk. And I have feelings..."

"Wait a minute. 'Was,' as in past tense?"

"No," said Rosemary. "Well, yes and no. I mean, he was away for a bit..."

"He goes away a lot, doesn't he?" He chuckled. "You know, I'm here all the time."

"I said it's *not* a competition."

"Still, it must leave you lonely."

"It does, a little," she admitted. "I don't mind being on my own. I've done it for a long time. I just don't know where I stand, exactly."

"He's a bit aloof, isn't he?" said Liam.

"I don't want to talk about my relationship with Burk with you. But I do feel a little guilty, like I shouldn't be spending time with you in this way."

"It's fine," said Liam with a shrug. "We're just friends. Friends having a nice picnic together."

"Thank you," said Rosemary, allowing her shoulders to relax. "I don't think I'm cut out for dating anyone, really, let alone multiple people."

"Well, I'm happy to be whatever you need me to be," said Liam. "I'll be your friend. I'll stand by you. I've got your back."

"That's really nice. I appreciate that. I could always do with more friends."

Liam smiled. "I just needed to know that I put myself out there. I let you know how I feel."

Rosemary frowned again. "Do *you* even know how you feel?"

"I've always held a candle for you, Rosey," said Liam. "And I always will. Maybe this isn't the right time. Maybe there'll never be a right time. Maybe there's somebody else for me, out there somewhere. But I needed to know that I'd said my piece."

Rosemary smiled at him. "This is all very mature and civilised."

"It is, isn't it?"

"I'm sure there is somebody out there for you," said Rosemary as Liam pulled out a thermos and teacups. She grinned at him. "Look, you're clearly the perfect man."

Seven

"What about this one?" Athena held up an emerald green gown.

Rosemary smiled. "Haven't you heard that if you wear green to a wedding Leprechauns come and steal away your fertility?"

"That doesn't sound too bad," Athena joked.

"Oh, forget it," said Rosemary. "Wear green. It's probably for the best if you don't have a magic baby anytime soon."

"It seems relatively unlikely," said Athena, putting the green dress back on the rack.

They were shopping at the Cobbleston mall, looking for outfits for Neve and Nesta's big day, which was coming up quite quickly.

"Maybe blue," Rosemary suggested, holding up a long, strappy number in sapphire with a slit up the side.

"If you want to go for the slutty-mum-look," said Athena.

"Hey!" Rosemary said. "Maybe I do."

Athena laughed. "Go on then, try it on."

Rosemary returned from the fitting rooms feeling glamorous. "What do you think?"

"Actually, the slutty-mum-look kind of suits you," Athena admitted. "Are you going to get it?"

"Maybe I will," said Rosemary. "Have you had any luck finding something?"

"I'm thinking of yellow," said Athena.

Her eyes glazed over into a dazed expression. Rosemary followed her teen's gaze to see she was staring at an attractive looking girl across the other side of the shop who was decidedly not Elise and therefore not her girlfriend.

"Athena!" Rosemary hissed. "Snap out of it."

"Oh, sorry." Athena shook herself.

"What's with you today? You keep turning your head to check out attractive people as they walk past."

"I might be a little bit ill or something."

Rosemary gave her a skeptical look. "What with?"

"I don't know!" Athena snapped. "Stop hassling me. What about you? Have you decided about Bermuda yet?"

"Nice change of subject, really subtle," said Rosemary. "And of course I have. I decided from the very first moment and my mind hasn't changed. We are absolutely not going."

"Oh, come on, Mum. I'm curious to know what goes on down there."

"Curiosity killed the cat," said Rosemary.

"While we wouldn't want anything to happen to glorious

little Serpentine, I'm sure she's at low risk in this situation. I don't think we should take her..."

"The answer is still no," said Rosemary.

"Why do you always do this?" Athena asked.

"Do what?"

"Bury your head in the sand at any possible change or sign of danger."

"Avoiding danger tends to be a good idea." Rosemary crossed her arms defensively.

"You're a grown woman - a powerful witch. You have avoidance issues."

"Who made you a shrink?" Rosemary asked. "Sometimes it's good to avoid things."

"Sometimes," said Athena. "Other times it just causes you more trouble."

"What is this really about?" Rosemary asked.

"I'm serious about the childhood issues," said Athena. "For a long time you let yourself be a victim of your whole life...of Dad's whims...a poverty of life. It's time to get over it. Stop reverting to stupid childlike behavior."

"You've got a bee in your bonnet," said Rosemary. "What's going on?"

"I just told you," said Athena. "This is not about me."

But her gaze was quickly captured by an attractive young man walking past the shop.

"Oh really?" Rosemary raised her eyebrows. Her daughter was acting rather erratically. And there was a bitterness in Athena's words that had settled in her. They had a ring of truth.

They finished their shopping and stopped in the food court for a quick bite to eat. Athena's words lingered in Rosemary's mind. She hated the idea of being a powerless victim. The thought made her reflect on her childhood, especially her parents and their strong beliefs. Being so immersed in their church, they'd taught her that she was powerless to a distant god and his devil nemesis.

Although she didn't want to hear it from her teen, she certainly didn't want to be a victim to life, either. *I'm a powerful witch. I'm not going to be a pathetic waste of space ever again.*

Eight

"You're doing it again."

"What?" Athena asked, taking in her mother's concerned look.

"You know," said Rosemary. "Checking people out as they walk past."

Athena took a sip of her soda and then ate last bite of her burger. Then she sighed, having run out of distractions. "I am being a bit weird aren't I?" she said.

"Do you want to talk about it?" Rosemary asked. "Is something wrong between you and Elise?"

"No, there's nothing wrong," said Athena. "Everything's wonderful. It's just, I don't know...I'm out of sorts. Maybe it's just teenage brain stuff."

"I think you're well beyond puberty. Do you think there could be something magical at play?"

Athena laughed. "Isn't there always? At least these days in

45

our lives..."

"Fair point," said Rosemary. "Just be vigilant in case we miss any signs of strange things happening."

"Strange things are always happening. It's time we just accept this is our life now...and there are so many good things about it."

"You're right," said Rosemary. "Things are nice and quiet. We should appreciate it while we can." She ate the last French fry and then looked up to see Athena staring at another stranger.

"You can control yourself!" said Rosemary. "Look at me."

Athena looked back to her mother.

"What is going on?"

"I might tell you if I knew," said Athena. "But honestly, I just feel weird."

"Okay, maybe it is just hormones." Rosemary sighed. "How is Elise, anyway?"

"Fine...amazing, actually. I'm supposed to be meeting her soon, remember?"

"I know. I'm glad you haven't forgotten in your...strangeness. Say hi for me. I'm so glad things are going well between you."

"So am I," said Athena. She took another sip of her drink and felt dread settling in on her. She couldn't help it. She had feelings, feelings all over the place.

She'd see a stranger walking past and be swamped by emotion, not just physical attraction but a wave of infatuation, and moment later she'd snap out of it and be back to herself. It was all enough to make her feel rather queasy, as if she was at sea on a rough day.

It all started with that minstrel...he must have done something to me.

Then again, a lot of other people had been there at the pub. She hadn't heard of any other strange effects. She hadn't had any particular interaction with him, either. Never spoken or touched. So perhaps that was just a coincidence and there was something else wrong with her. Whatever it was, she hoped it ended soon.

"What's up?" Elise said as Athena met her at the ice cream parlor in Myrtlewood later in the day. "You seem stressed."

Athena sighed. "I don't know how to explain it. I just feel really weird."

She noticed their other friends were already inside, sitting at a booth.

"I hope you don't mind us gatecrashing," said Ash, as they entered the shop.

Athena turned towards her friends and stared at Felix.

"Uhh...Earth to Athena," he said. "What's gotten into you?"

Athena shook her head and caught a glimpse of an anguished expression on Elise's face. "Athena?"

"Sorry, I'm not feeling very well. I've got to go."

"Wait," said Elise. "Are you okay?"

"I'll be fine. I must have eaten something funny at the mall. I've got to go home now."

She ran out the shop, her heart racing. She couldn't get the look on Elise's face out of her head after she'd seen the way Athena was looking at their friend.

She felt dizzy and confused, but there was no one she felt comfortable talking to. Not about this.

Nine

"You always surprise me," said Rosemary.

"What did you expect?" Burk asked as they drove down a country farm track through an enormous field of wheat.

"Well, the last date you took me on was at a very swanky magical restaurant and now we're on a farm."

Burk grinned. "I like to shake things up a little."

"And it's still technically daylight."

"Yes," he agreed. "But I have a sun-proof car and I want to watch the sunset with you."

The late afternoon sun beamed down on them as a cool breeze rushed through the open window.

"I suppose it is rather lovely," said Rosemary, looking around and taking in the wide open space with the distant rise of hills.

Burk opened a bottle of champagne and poured it into a glass.

Rosemary took a sip. It tasted crisp and refreshing and smooth.

He checked his watch. "Now it should be safe."

"For what?"

"For this."

She watched as Burk slid on sunglasses and got out of the car.

Rosemary's heartrate rose in panic.

"It's okay," he said. "I've got extremely strong sunscreen on and the sun is less potent at this time of the day."

Rosemary watched cautiously as he walked around to her side of the car and opened the door for her, before offering her a hand.

She got out of the car, relieved that he hadn't melted or burst into dust or anything.

Burk spread out a picnic blanket and retrieved a basket from his car and then laid out an elaborate spread.

"All for me?" she asked, admiring the fancy cheeses, breads, and other delicious things.

"I'm afraid so. It wouldn't do me much good."

"It seems a little unfair," said Rosemary.

"Don't worry. I've already eaten."

She choked on her champagne.

"It still makes you uncomfortable, doesn't it?" He laughed, but Rosemary noticed a serious note in his voice.

"Just remember, I'm slowly adjusting."

"Good. Cheers!"

Rosemary held up her champagne glass. Burk clinked an empty one.

"Sorry."

He smiled. "I've been around a long time, Rosemary. It's pretty hard for you to offend me at this point."

"Well, given my track record, we might be a match made in heaven, then. I'm pretty sure I've offended half the town at one point or another and I've only been here half a year or so."

Burk laughed. "You're such a fascinating woman," he said, stroking a stray strand of hair behind her ear.

Rosemary felt a swooning in her abdomen. Despite not being entirely on board with everything vampiric yet, she did have feelings for this particular being and his gorgeous eyes and his beautiful soft hair.

Before she knew it they were locked in a passionate kiss and Rosemary felt everything else inside her heating up and craving more.

The kiss, which was a really good one, ended eventually and Rosemary took another sip of champagne.

"Oh, this sunset!" she said as the sky deepened into more tones of orange, pink, purple, and yellow. They watched the beautiful sky.

"It's why I brought you here."

"This is why you brought me to a field?" Rosemary said. "You get a similar view of wide open spaces if you go to the beach, you know."

"I've been told that sand gets in the way of a good picnic."

Rosemary narrowed her eyes. "How many other women have you been taking on picnics?"

Burk laughed. "It's funny you should ask that after your date with Liam."

Rosemary shook her head. "I told you, he might have had designs on a date, but we're just friends."

"Well, in that case let me assure you that this is the first time I've had a picnic in a very long while," Burk said. "There aren't many women that I find fascinating enough."

The evening passed like a glorious dream.

They talked about themselves and their lives. Rosemary shared her worries about Athena and learned more about Burk.

"Are you ever going to tell me how it was that you became a vampire?" she asked causally, though she expected it was a sensitive subject.

Burk's expression darkened and Rosemary wished she could take back her words.

"My brother and I..." He cleared his throat. "We were merchants. I looked up to him back then, but he was always a rogue, looking out for any way to line his pockets."

Rosemary nodded and kept her tongue firmly between her teeth so as not to interrupt.

"We were dealing in silks but ran afoul of Henry II's men in Verona. They stabbed us and left us to die in the street. That's when my sire found us. He says he had been looking for vampire progeny but did not want to take human lives unfairly."

"That sounds very noble for an ancient vampire," said Rosemary sagely.

Burk nodded. "We begged him to save us, and he did. We became family."

"It's interesting to me that vampires have this concept of family that isn't about genetics as much as...erm...transmission?"

Burk cleared his throat, and then coughed. Then he began

laughing hysterically. "Your way of phrasing things always surprises me, Rosemary Thorn."

Rosemary frowned. "Am I really that silly?"

"No, you're spectacular. As for family. It's not quite in the same way as human mortals."

She looked into his eyes and caught a glimpse of something raw and primal and ancient that went to the heart of the very nature of his being. It was terrifying, but also beautiful. And it only made her want more.

"What's it like?" she asked. "Never going old...never dying?"

"We can still die, of course."

"Please don't," said Rosemary with a smile. "I'm starting to quite like you."

He laughed and kissed her again.

"As for your question," he said, "it's hard to explain what it's like. It was so long ago that I was a normal human being that I can't really compare. However, I think time works differently for me. It's more fleeting, except in moments like this where it seems to stretch out forever."

Rosemary felt warmth spread through her chest as the final beams of sunlight sank down behind the distant hills.

"Now it's time for us to turn around," Burk said in his silky voice.

"Turn around?"

"Yes. Turn around and watch this."

She turned to see an enormous harvest moon rising over the wheatfield.

"Oh wow."

Burk simply smiled, his face unnervingly handsome in the moonlight.

"Now I understand why you brought me here." Rosemary grinned.

"I thought you might enjoy it."

Rosemary reached for Burk again and kissed him, thinking about her dreams before the solstice...the raunchy, steamy dreams involving Burk, where he could find her on the dance floor and ferry her away into some beautiful natural landscape to make love to her.

Of course the solstice didn't quite go that way. Everything always seemed to be interrupted. *Not tonight*, she hoped, getting lost in another mind melting kiss.

It was such a nice break from the chaos. Rosemary reflected that life would be perfect if there wasn't so much danger and drama.

Being with a vampire didn't sound like a normal quiet life, but deep within her she felt a knowing sense growing.

Rosemary really did want to be with him. She wanted Burk in a serious way...even though he survived on blood and was practically immortal.

She wanted this body. She wanted to feel the sensations of him all over her...It had been such a long time.

Burk pulled back from the kiss. "Wait."

Rosemary looked at him. "What?"

"I was questioning...what is it that you want, Rosemary?"

"Right now?" she asked, a goading tease in her voice. She trailed a finger down from his bottom lip to his chest.

"I mean, in general, what is it you're really looking for right now in your life?"

Rosemary took a deep breath. She wasn't about to admit the depth of her feelings to Burk. Not just yet.

It was only their second date, after all.

"A nice quiet life," Rosemary said.

Just then, a scream tore through the air around them.

Burk's eyes went wide.

"Oh no, I jinxed it!" Rosemary said.

They began to run towards the sound of the scream.

Burk was far faster, of course. By the time Rosemary reached him, he was crouched over a woman, her body splayed, creating an indentation in the wheat around her.

"She's a vampire," Burk said. "She's barely alive."

"Do you know her?" Rosemary asked.

He shook his head.

"What happened?" Rosemary looked towards the woman and noticed a bright purple feather piercing her chest. "That looks familiar."

It was almost exactly like the feather Rosemary had found at Finn's Creek several months before after a little girl had gone missing.

Burk's expression darkened. "It's a message from the fae, or someone pretending to be them."

Rosemary nodded. "What does it mean?"

"I don't know."

"Is it too late to save her?" Rosemary asked.

"I'm afraid so," he replied as the woman's body burst into a cloud of dust.

Rosemary gasped. "I suppose it is now."

They were both silent for a moment before Rosemary asked, "Do you know what happened?"

Burk stood up and brushed off his pants, a dark look in his eyes. "It was magic. Someone attacked her...stopped her heart."

"Oh, how awful. What does this mean?"

"Bermuda," said Burk.

"You don't think it was them?" Rosemary asked.

"No. Rosemary, do you know why it is that you're being summoned to Bermuda?"

"Of course not. Why do you think those snobby witches would go and do a sensible thing like explaining things?"

Burk let out a long slow breath.

"What is it?" Rosemary asked.

"I've been summoned too."

"You have?" Rosemary asked. "Why?"

"As an emissary, I suppose."

"A messenger for vampire kind?" Rosemary asked.

"In a matter of speaking."

"Okay, why?" Rosemary asked. "What kind of message would you deliver?"

"I have no idea," said Burk. "I suspect it's all highly political, but this incident makes me much more concerned."

"How is this related to Bermuda?" Rosemary asked. "What does the murder of a vampire by the fae have to do with fancy-pants witch officials?"

"It's a message," said Burk. "A message for me. Someone is warning me to back off."

"A bit full of yourself, aren't you?" Rosemary said. "Assuming it's all about you."

"A murdered vampire like this is uncommon," said Burk.

"Oh goddess," said Rosemary. "Sorry for being so insensitive. Did you know her?"

"No," said Burk. "Which, in itself, is unusual given I know most of my kind for miles around. Besides, someone went to great effort to set this up in the middle of nowhere so close to where we were picnicking. They took a lot of care to ensure she stayed alive long enough for us to see her."

"Do we call the authorities?" Rosemary asked. "The police?"

"She was a vampire. The Council will handle it," said Burk. "If they have any record of her they may be able to identify her through the traces of dust left behind."

"What do the vampire council know about all this stuff with Bermuda?"

"I have no idea," said Burk. "The only thing they said when I told them of the invitation was that it could be a chance for peace between magical beings and that I should go."

"Peace?" Rosemary laughed. "Fat chance of that ever happening around here."

"If it's true," said Burk, "then going to Bermuda could be your chance for a quiet life."

"There's no way in Hades," said Rosemary.

Ten

"What's up, my dear?" Marjie asked as she entered the chocolate shop.

Rosemary had her head resting on her hands, which were pressed against the counter.

"I tried to ask her that already," Papa Jack called from the kitchen where he was busy stirring a batch of passionfruit truffle mixture. "She said it was nothing."

"But it's clearly something," said Marjie.

"That's what I said," Papa Jack replied.

"Oh, sweetheart," Marjie said, patting Rosemary gently on the head. "Is it something with the shop?"

"Not at all," said Rosemary, pulling herself up to standing. "The shop is going great. We've had loads of customers. I'm surprised something in my life has gone off without a hitch."

"Ahh," said Marjie knowingly. "What's going on with Athena, then?"

"How did you know?" Rosemary asked.

"It's obvious you care more about that girl than life itself," said Marjie. "Has she gotten into trouble again?"

"Not exactly," said Rosemary. "I don't know what's going on. I wish I did."

Marjie sighed, clearly taking the hint that the matter was a sensitive one. She lowered her voice. "Is it a matter of the heart, dear?"

"In a round-about way," Rosemary said. "She's been acting very odd. At first I thought it would pass, but it only seems to be getting worse."

Just then, little Zoya popped her head out from behind the counter. "Can I help you, Mrs Marjie?" she asked. "Any chocolates for today?"

"It's ten in the morning," said Marjie, but upon seeing the crestfallen expression on Zoya's face, she added, "But never too early for chocolate. I'll just have one little Irish cream, dear."

Zoya beamed and served her the truffle in a little purple paper bag.

"Wonderful service!" said Marjie. "And you might want to know that Una is at the park with the foundling children. You can go and play with them when you need a break from all your hard work."

Zoya looked towards her grandfather excitedly. "Can I?"

"The park just around the corner?" he asked. "Of course you can. I can see it from the back window of the shop! And yes, there are a bunch of kids there. Go play!"

Zoya dashed out of the shop.

"Good idea," said Rosemary.

"Yes, thank you," said Papa Jack. "I've been wondering how to keep her occupied while I work, at least until school starts up for the year. I tried to suggest the park to her earlier, but she was too shy."

"It makes a difference if she knows someone there, I suppose," said Rosemary.

"I'll save this for later," said Marjie, popping the purple truffle bag into her purse. "But back to the matter at hand. Have you thought of asking Dain about Athena?"

"Oh, bother Dain," said Rosemary. "What would he know about parenting?"

"Perhaps not very much at all," said Marjie. "But I'd say he'd know a lot more than either of us do about being a fae teenager."

Rosemary sighed. "You have a point. I just feel so helpless. Yesterday after our shopping trip Athena went to meet some friends but came back straight away and went to her room feeling weird, only she insisted it wasn't a physical illness. This morning she insisted she wasn't going to leave the house all day. I felt bad leaving her alone. Come to think of it, maybe Una knows something that would help."

"Why don't you call both of them – Una and Dain – and see if they can give you any more information on what could be the matter?"

"That sounds infinitely sensible," said Rosemary, though she didn't feel too excited about seeking parenting advice from one of the most erratic fathers she'd ever come across. "I might just do that."

"And go home," said Papa Jack. "Be with your girl if when she needs you."

"I don't want to leave you in the lurch," said Rosemary. "I don't want to lose my star employee."

"Hey, I might not be able to make the most magical truffles yet, but you know I'm fine with everything else."

"It looks like you're doing well in the kitchen," said Marjie, "but let me know if you'd like a few magical lessons. Kitchen witchery is my specialty, after all."

Papa Jack smiled. "That would be excellent. My son, Arjun, was the real magical genius in our family...before."

The warmth faded from his expression for a moment, and Rosemary's heart went out to him. To lose a child...and so mysteriously.

"Your son," said Marjie. "Zoya's father."

Papa Jack nodded. "He and his wife were out for a walk while I was babysitting Zoya a few years ago and they just vanished. That's all I know," said Papa Jack sadly. "The police have given up looking for them. I've been taking care of the little one ever since. She's doing so well, considering, but we both miss her parents... every single day. The pain never stops."

"How absolutely devastating!" said Marjie.

Rosemary put a comforting hand on his shoulder. "Let's see what we can do to find out what happened." She carefully chose her words. She couldn't bear to give him false hope of getting his only child back, but some of the warmth returned to his eyes at her words.

"You're a star, Rosemary Thorn," said Papa Jack. "But for now, you just go home. We have plenty of stock and you have nothing to worry about. I love it here."

Rosemary smiled at her friend. "Okay, if you insist."

Athena only responded in one syllable words from her bed when Rosemary checked on her, upon returning to Thorn Manor.

Teenagers! Rosemary clomped downstairs in frustration, retrieved her phone from her handbag, and sent messages to both Una and Dain.

Neither responded immediately, but Rosemary suspected Una was still busy with the children in the park, and Dain...well, who ever knew about him?

She made herself a cup of tea and drank it while pondering Athena's odd behaviour the day before. Just as she finished her first cup and was staring at the dregs, considering whether it was worth learning to read tea leaves, the doorbell rang.

"Dain?" Rosemary said, slightly surprised to see him there so soon. He was wearing a rather smart shirt and new-looking jeans, even his hair seemed more groomed than usual, making him look unfairly handsome.

"Hey, you said you wanted to talk about Athena," said Dain. "Why do you look so shocked?"

"I expected a message in a few hours," said Rosemary. "Not such a prompt response."

"Are you implying I don't care about our daughter?" Dain asked defensively. "Or is it more that you still think I'm a total loser who can't get his act together?"

"Well..." said Rosemary. "You have seemed a bit more mature of late, I admit, but I'm still getting used to it."

"Fair enough," said Dain, seeming to be no longer offended, only slightly sad. "Everything has been different since you solved my cream addiction. But I suppose it takes a while to show that someone's really changed their stripes."

"Something like that," said Rosemary. "So..."

"Athena?" Dain prompted. "What's going on?"

"She's been acting very odd."

Dain looked extremely concerned, and then enraged. "Has someone hurt her? I'll go after them. Teach them a lesson!"

"Erm, I'm not sure," said Rosemary. "Maybe settle down on the macho revenge fantasy until we can figure this out?"

"Oh, right," said Dain. "Tell me the details."

"Well, she told me she's had strange tingling sensations and has been feeling woozy and behaving weirdly."

Rosemary filled him in on the travelling minstrel debacle.

"I'll kill him!" Dain said, fuming.

"Settle down!" Rosemary instructed in her best 'mum' voice. "I haven't told you all the details yet."

"There's more? What else has the musician prick done?"

"Not him," said Rosemary. "We went to the mall and Athena kept...uhh..."

"What?"

"She kept checking people out as they walked past, staring at them as if she was smitten."

To Rosemary's shock, Dain began to laugh.

"What?" she asked.

Dain tried to respond, but continued laughing so hard he couldn't get a word out. Eventually he managed to slow down enough, aided by Rosemary's glaring, to ask, "Were they staring right back at her?"

"I guess," said Rosemary, and then it dawned on her. "Oh...oh no!"

"I'm afraid so," said Dain.

"She's just like you!"

Dain broke into hysterical laughter again.

"It's not funny!" Rosemary said. "This is...just not Athena - not her personality at all."

"It'll pass," said Dain. "Well, at least parts of it."

Rosemary glared daggers. "Athena!" she yelled towards the stairs. "Get down here right now! Your father has some explaining to do!"

"I'm going to put on some more tea," said Rosemary. "We'll need it."

"No milk for me, thanks," said Dain.

"That goes without saying," Rosemary replied as she went to the kitchen to put the kettle on.

They heard a muffled groan and then the sound of Athena's footsteps as she made her way down.

"What's all this about, then?" Athena asked. "You disturbed me from a nice nap."

"Take a seat," said Rosemary, gesturing to the kitchen table.

"Oh fine," said Athena. "But this better be good."

"Your father has some information on your present situation," Rosemary said as the kettle began to boil.

"Mum!" said Athena. "You didn't tell him?!"

"A little," said Rosemary.

"But that's private!" Athena folded her arms, looking incredibly unimpressed.

"It's just as well that I did," Rosemary continued. "You're going to want to hear what he's got to say."

"Alright then, Dad," said Athena grumpily. "Out with it."

Dain took a deep breath and then his smile spread wide.

"Congratulations, darling," he said. "You're coming of age as a fae!"

At that moment, the kettle began to whistle loudly, blocking out the long chain of expletives that issued from Athena's mouth.

Rosemary removed the kettle and made the tea. There was silence for a moment while they all digested the situation.

Dain looked happy and proud, while Athena brooded.

Rosemary's anxiety raced in her chest as she carried the tea tray to the table.

"Okay," she said. "Let's start at the beginning. Dain, you've always had a certain...way with the ladies."

"I told you I couldn't help it," said Dain. "It's just fae charm. It starts off rather...mutual."

"As in?" Athena asked.

Dain smiled apologetically. "As in you kind of fall in love with random strangers just as much as they fall in love with you."

"It's not real love though," said Athena, looking mildly disgusted. "It's more like motion sickness."

"It peaks around the time we come of age," Dain explained.

"And you didn't think to warn me?!" said Athena, outraged.

"It didn't cross my mind that you'd be affected," Dain said earnestly. "You're as much human as you are fae. After all, the cream has no power over you."

"This is awful!" said Athena. "What about Elise? How am I

supposed to have a healthy relationship if I'm falling into magical fae infatuation left, right, and centre?"

"That's a tricky situation, love," said Rosemary. "Your best bet is to be completely honest with her."

Dain laughed. "Personally, I'd recommend going away until it wears off or only hanging out with your girlfriend when other people aren't around."

Rosemary glared at him. "That is not good advice for a parent to give a teenager," she grumbled.

"It's all so hopeless," Athena said, burying her head in her hands on the table and partially spilling her untouched tea.

"Don't worry," said Dain, awkwardly patting his daughter on the head. "It will wear off."

Athena looked up hopefully. "How long?" she asked.

"Mine started to fade a few months after turning seventeen," Dain offered casually.

"Months!" said Athena, aghast. "Months! I can't believe this."

"Yes, right around the time I met your mother," Dain added.

"Oh, and that turned out so well," said Athena bitterly.

Rosemary bit her lower lip. Athena had a point.

"Yes, well, I stopped having all the wayward feelings at least. It didn't stop the girls from loving me...or boys for that matter, or solve any of my other problems."

"So," said Athena, as if slowly thinking things over. Then, bursting with anger she continued. "You're saying random people will *still* find me enchantingly attractive! Gross!"

"Hey. I've got it under control now," said Dain. "More or less."

"How?" Rosemary asked.

"Yes, how?" said Athena. "Can you teach me?"

"It's like a muscle you can grow," said Dain. "Some fae find it easier to channel away the energy through some kind of craft."

"Are you suggesting I take up knitting?!" Athena demanded, sitting up straight again. "Because you know I'm not into that."

"Something creative," said Dain. "Maybe a type of art? The theory is that fae charm is really all a kind of creative energy and that doing something like...oh I don't know, drawing, singing, or poetry...can keep that energy busy, sink it into something other than attractive passersby."

"It's seems like a stretch," said Athena. "I'm not really the artsy type, and any poetry I've attempted turns out so cringey I can't even look at it."

"Worth a try, love," said Rosemary encouragingly. "But I do think you should be up front with Elise about it all. Deception will only lead to heartache."

"You're probably right." Athena pouted and then she slumped back over the table again, pressing her cheek against the wood. "Oh, but it's hopeless. She feels insecure already over the situation with Finnigan...and now I've gone and..."

"What?" Rosemary asked.

"It's too embarrassing to say," said Athena.

Rosemary frowned, desperate to know what was bothering her daughter so much, but somehow managed to restrain herself from intrusive questioning.

"It'll all work out," said Dain, still sounding buoyant. "And anyway, you're much more stable than me. You'll handle it all brilliantly. I'm...I'm proud of you."

Athena groaned.

Rosemary smiled sympathetically at Dain. He seemed genuinely happy for Athena's coming of age as a fae, despite her reaction. Dain wasn't hitting the right notes, clearly, but he was making an effort and being uncharacteristically sincere.

"I'm going back to bed," said Athena, picking herself up off the table and wandering out of the room.

"Well..." said Rosemary.

"That went well," said Dain ironically. He frowned.

"It's a relief to know what's going on at least." Rosemary poured them both more tea.

"At least with that particular situation," said Dain, scratching his chin.

"What else is happening in your world?" Rosemary asked, curious.

"I..." said Dain, straightening up his posture and gesticulating grandly, "have been summoned to Bermuda by the Arch Magistrate himself."

Rosemary laughed.

"What?" said Dain. "I thought you'd be impressed."

"By Bermuda?" Rosemary raised her eyebrows incredulously. "No way. I'm not interested in witching hierarchical snobbery."

Dain laughed. "I knew there was a reason I liked you."

Rosemary glared at him. "No flirting," she said firmly. "But for the record, Athena and I have been summonsed too."

"Oh really?" Dain asked, his interest piqued.

"I'm afraid so."

"The whole fam."

"Yep," said Rosemary. "One big family outing that I'm not going on. And neither is Athena."

Dain gulped down his tea and then looked at Rosemary questioningly. "Aren't you curious?" he asked.

"About Bermuda?" Rosemary shook her head. "It all smells like trouble to me, and we've had quite enough of that. I want peace and quiet."

"Funny you should say that," said Dain as he rose from the table and began to show himself out.

"Why?" Rosemary asked, following him to the door.

"There have been murmurings..."

"Rumours, you mean?"

Dain furrowed his brows. "Maybe more than that. The word is that some kind of formal truce could be in the works."

"A truce?"

"Between fae and witches, maybe vampires too."

"Oh," said Rosemary. Her mind raced through everything she knew about magical politics. There had been wars between vampires and fae, and witches had put up protections on the veil between the realms so that fae couldn't easily cross over. It was clearly far more convoluted than that, but she hadn't sought to learn more. She'd been quite busy enough with her regular levels of magical chaos. Her mind darted to the dead vampire girl and her conversation with Burk in the field. "I suppose not everyone is so keen on a truce."

Dain gave her an odd look. "What do you know?"

She filled him in on the unexpected interruption to her date.

"So you're still seeing the bloodsucker then?" said Dain.

Rosemary gave him a little push. "Oh, get out!"

"But seriously," said Dain. "He's right. It sounds like a message to the vampires to say away from the fae. Someone wants us to remain enemies."

"What else do you know about this truce?" Rosemary asked. "It's not like we're properly at war anymore."

"Some kind of formal agreement between the 'ruling' magical species."

Rosemary laughed. "So snobbish!"

"Snobby, it may be," said Dain. "But perhaps tolerating a little snobbery is a small price to pay for global magical peace."

And with that, he bowed and made his exit.

Rosemary stood there for a moment, staring at the door, pondering those words.

If I want peace, then maybe this is the way to do it. Plus, it could mean more time spent with a rather aloof vampire...

Eleven

Athena lay in bed, staring blankly at the ceiling.

This was the worst possible timing. She and Elise had just gotten to a really good place with their relationship after the ups and downs of the Summer Festival, and things were going so well.

Now Athena had to worry about potentially falling for every second stranger on the street.

She knew she had to try to figure out how she could keep something like this concealed, as her father had suggested. But that seemed far too complicated.

"If only we could go to Bermuda," Athena muttered to herself. "Until the worst of this settles down, at least."

She held a pillow over her face and screamed.

When the tears came she wasn't sure where they were from, exactly. She felt more angry and frustrated than anything. But it did also seem quite unfair.

It wasn't her choice to be fae. She certainly never asked for this particular magical power if indeed that's what it could be described as.

There was a knock at the door.

"Are you alright, love?" Rosemary called out. "I thought I heard something."

"I'm fine. I just need to be alone."

"Okay," said Rosemary. "But I brought you some soup. I'll just leave it outside."

Athena's tummy rumbled in response, and she realized she hadn't eaten all day.

"Actually, I'm starved. Do you mind bringing it in?"

Rosemary opened the door and crossed the room to place the tray carefully on the end of Athena's bed.

"Oh love, it's not fair, is it?"

"Not at all," said Athena. "Wait, what are you wearing?"

Rosemary looked down at the dark purple top and black jeans she'd thrown on that morning. "What do you mean?"

She glanced at Athena who looked mortified and happened to be in almost exactly the same outfit, just with longer sleeves and a slightly different cut.

Rosemary laughed. "I suppose I can't be so unfashionable now."

"Or I'm in a worse funk than I realised."

"Hey – matching outfits are cute."

"Sure, when you're five!" Athena felt tears prick her eyes and that only made her feel more ridiculous."

Rosemary smiled sympathetically. "Don't worry. We'll get through this. We always do."

"Do you think maybe we could just go away for a while?" Athena pleaded. "It doesn't have to be Bermuda. It could be anywhere. Just for a few months until I'm more...under control."

Rosemary shrugged apologetically. "It would be really bad timing for the shop. I could probably manage a few days at most."

"Fair enough," said Athena. "I suppose it's too much to ask to save your only daughter from a relationship nightmare."

"You really should tell Elise, love," said Rosemary. "It's the only fair thing to do. Put yourself in her shoes. Wouldn't you want to know?"

"I guess. But things have been a bit tense. Elise gets insecure and sometimes thinks...I don't know what she thinks. She worries that I don't like her that much. And this is only going to make it worse."

"Believe me," said Rosemary. "It'll be far worse if she doesn't know what's going on. At least if she has all the information she can make up her mind for herself rather than speculating."

"I suppose you're right," said Athena. "Only...how much worse is this going to get?"

Rosemary patted her daughter on the shoulder. "If it makes it easier I could go back to being incredibly of protective again. Keep you on a short leash."

"Actually, I can't believe I'm saying this." Athena sat up and pulled the tray of soup and toast towards her. "That's not the worst idea."

"Now I'm really worried," said Rosemary. "I never thought you'd agree to anything like that."

Athena laughed. "I don't like being out of control of my body. That's all."

"I don't blame you," said Rosemary. "Neither do I. It's horrible. But I have an idea."

"What is it?" Athena asked, not sounding too hopeful.

"Well, you remember when I was acting particularly frantic and erratically and granny gave me this pendant?" Rosemary gestured to the emerald necklace she wore.

Athena blinked and rubbed her eyes. "Do you think it might help?"

"It's worth a try, isn't it?"

"And you're going to give it to me?"

"Lend it," said Rosemary. "But be careful. It's a priceless family heirloom. Don't let anyone else take it or anything. You know, most people wouldn't be able to handle the magic. It made Sherry loopy."

"Do you think I can handle it?" Athena asked. "It might just make me worse."

Rosemary bit her lower lip and frowned. "I think it's worth a try. And hey, if you do seem to be getting worse, I'll monitor the situation and take it off you."

"Okay," Athena said. "Hand it over...please."

Rosemary removed the necklace and placed her around Athena's neck.

The clasp snapped into place like a magnet.

"Oh, it feels nice," said Athena.

Rosemary watched her suspiciously for a moment.

"Not like a drug or anything," said Athena. "Sort of cool and calming."

"That's how it feels for me, too. I'm not sure I'm totally prepared to be without it. But in this case, yours is the greater need."

"Thanks, Mum," said Athena, giving her mother a hug. "And thanks for the soup too."

"Somebody's got to look after you. What else is a mother for?"

"Well, sometimes they're for driving me up the wall," said Athena playfully. "But right now I admit you're rather good to have around."

Rosemary gave her daughter a squeeze. "I'm glad it's helping. What do you think about your father's suggestion?"

"What, about being deceptive and mischievous?" Athena asked.

"No, not that one. I was talking about his idea that you could channel that wild love machine fae energy into something creative."

Athena blew a raspberry in the air, making a deflated balloon sound with her lips. "I suppose I could give it a whirl. I've never really been all that crafty."

"Granny had some painting supplies in one of the cupboards downstairs. I could bring them up for you if you like," Rosemary suggested.

"I'll give it a go," said Athena.

"All right, finish your food and I'll be back soon."

Athena ate the rest of her soup, enjoying the simple flavors, especially given how hungry she was. She was just finishing the dregs when Rosemary reemerged from the doorway carrying a stack of canvases and a few other boxes of art things.

"There's quite a lot of stuff here actually," said Rosemary. "But then again, Granny was into all sorts of arts and crafts. I'll put them over on the desk for you."

"Thanks Mum."

"I'll let you rest now and check up on you later."

Rosemary left and Athena collapsed back into the bed. She thought she'd be exhausted enough to sleep, but all of a sudden the painting supplies were calling to her.

She got up and wandered over to her desk, choosing one of the canvases and a little box of oil paints. She'd never done any painting aside from the obligatory school art sessions. Right now this seemed to be exactly what she needed. She picked out the tube of sky blue paint and began to experiment.

Twelve

Rosemary was almost finished setting up the Lughnasa themed display in the front window of the chocolate shop. She smiled as she admired the white chocolate sun, tinted yellow, that Papa Jack had helped her hang that morning, above the little golden truffles shaped like sheaths of wheat, and ears of corn, across from the caramel chocolate honey pots and tiny loaves of bread made with puffed fondant. She arranged the final pieces, a pair of over-sized chocolate honey bees.

"It looks brilliant!" said Papa Jack, popping out from the kitchen to admire their handiwork.

"Thanks for all your help," said Rosemary, giving him a quick hug.

She carried on around the shop, cleaning the various surfaces. Several customers had just left after enthusiastically enjoying their hot chocolate beverages, and the shop was quiet except for Papa Jack humming happily away as he cleaned the kitchen.

Rosemary was starting to feel like she was getting her groove back after taking off the necklace the day before. It had thrown her for the first few hours and she'd had a restless night without nearly enough sleep.

By the morning she'd adjusted. Aside from her tiredness and worries about Athena, she still felt a little bit more unstable than when she was wearing it. But she figured it was good to know she didn't need it. The necklace was a crutch, even if it was a beautiful family heirloom as well.

Athena was still at home. She'd been laying low for a couple of days and Rosemary was sure she hadn't explained the situation to Elise. Rosemary was sure that being honest about what was going on was the best plan. Alarm bells were ringing that keeping secrets like this would only lead to heartbreak, but she also knew that it was important to give her daughter time to make her own decisions.

After all, this was a sickness of one kind or another, at least in Athena's experience of it. She needed to process.

Rosemary was happy to see that Athena had started painting and seemed to be enjoying it. She only hoped it had the effect that Dain suggested of soaking up the infatuated energy, curtailing it somehow.

Just as she finished wiping the last table, the bell rang over the door.

Rosemary turned to see none other than Elamina Bracewell-Thorn entering the building.

"Oh, Rosemary," said Elamina, with a prim expression. "What a quaint little shop you have here. How charming." She drew out the word charming in a way that made Rosemary wish she'd opted for the magical trap door and other 'security' options the builder had proposed. She'd quite like to snap her fingers and send Elamina careening down to a cobwebby basement.

"Hello, cousin. What are you doing here?"

"Pleased to see me, I see," said Elamina, with an ironic raise of her eyebrow.

"As usual," said Rosemary, plastering on a fake smile. Two could play at this game. "What do you want?"

"I've been informed that you're invited to Bermuda." Elamina's voice became more tense. "By the Arch Magistrate herself." She stressed the syllables in such a way that Rosemary wondered if her cousin was totally going to lose her stuffing for a change.

"Herself?"

"Yes."

"Oh," said Rosemary. "I did receive an invitation and I threw it out. The little top hat man came back again and insisted. Quite a pain, really."

"You...Threw. It. Out." Elamina struggled with the words. A scandalous look on her face.

"Yeah," said Rosemary casually. "This might be your world, but it's not mine. I don't know exactly why you've got me invited to that fancy place."

"Believe me, I had nothing to do with it," Elamina snapped. "If it were up to me, you would be kept as far away as possible. However, given the circumstances..."

"What circumstances?" said Rosemary. "All I hear are rumours. Jeremiah, whatever his name is..."

"You mean Reginald?"

"Yeah, that's the one," said Rosemary. "He implied there's a huge amount of secrecy."

"Of course there is! There *must* be with the matters of high office."

"Well, you can get as high as you like. I'm perfectly comfortable down here on earth with my lowly, quaint little life." Rosemary smiled.

"If only it were that simple," said Elamina bitterly.

"Let me make it simple for you. You can count me out. I will stay as far away from this as possible. And you should be pleased. After all, you said it yourself - you don't want me involved."

"Be that as it may," said Elamina. "You've been summoned and you must attend."

"What if I don't want to?" Rosemary asked, leaning against the table.

"You must."

"And if I don't?"

"There will be consequences," said Elamina. "Why else do you think I trekked all the way out to this nonsense little village? Rosemary, this is serious."

"You're saying these people will attack me for not going to their stupid meeting? Doesn't sound very civilized."

"No, don't be ridiculous," said Elamina. "Your safety will be ensured."

"Oh, so they'll just kidnap me?" said Rosemary. "Is that what you're implying?"

"You may be...detained," Elamina said carefully. "If you're obstinate enough to continue to refuse. We are talking about the witching parliament here, not just your standard regional magical authority. This matter is serious."

Rosemary scoffed. "If it's so serious they'd better tell me what it's about."

"You're impossible!" Elamina threw her hands in the air and stormed out of the shop.

"What's got her in a tizzy?" said Papa Jack, coming out from the kitchen.

Rosemary laughed. "Actually that's about as much of a tizzy I've ever seen my cousin in. She's usually very cool."

"She seems a little elitist. She rich?"

"Oh, yes. Very rich and very powerful. And she can't stand me."

"Why come and visit you then?" Papa Jack asked.

"You didn't overhear the conversation?"

He shook his head. "Only the louder fragments."

Rosemary sighed. "It's all about the stupid invitation to the witching parliament in Bermuda. Apparently, if I don't go they might detain me...whatever that means. I bet it's an empty threat."

"I see," said Papa Jack. "If you don't want to go, you don't go. I'm sure you know what you're talking about. A woman like you knows your own will. You know what's important to you."

"I do," said Rosemary. "And I really don't want to go, personally. The problem is, it might backfire on me...or it could even be that the trip is worthwhile if what Dain said was true."

"What's that?" Papa Jack rubbed his chin. "If you don't mind me asking."

"Something about a truce between the big guns of the magical world to stop the fae and vampires from fighting."

"That sounds too political," said Papa Jack. "You'd be best to stay away in my opinion. Don't get sucked in."

"My thoughts exactly," said Rosemary. "I've got no idea why they'd need me, of all people."

"And you've got quite enough to deal with in Myrtlewood." Papa Jack patted her on the back.

"True, though it's been so peaceful around here lately, aside from the situation with Athena, which has turned out to be kind of magical growing pains."

Papa Jack smiled and nodded and then returned to the kitchen, and Rosemary continued packing up for the day. Things had indeed been calm across the township and she really wanted more than anything to keep it that way, but something told her she wouldn't be so lucky.

Thirteen

Rosemary returned from work the next day to find the front door open.

"Athena!" she called out.

She stepped cautiously inside, her hands up, ready to use magic, and came across a second curious sight.

Two travelling cases were popped up in the hallway.

"Through here," Athena called.

"What's going on?" Rosemary walked towards the kitchen and the sound of Athena's voice.

She stopped. Two familiar faces sat either side of the kitchen table, smiling at her, wearing their customary matching blue polyester tracksuits.

"Oh," said Rosemary, remembering the rather garbled phone message she'd received with a sinking sensation in her gut. "Mum and Dad. You came to visit?"

"That's right," said Athena. "I was just making them some tea."

Rosemary noted the plastic smile on her teen daughter's face.

"Such a lovely girl," said Rosemary's mother, Mariana, brushing her short greying hair from her forehead.

"Yes indeed," said Rosemary's father, Gerald, who wasn't in the least like his mother, her dear Granny. "We were just saying how Athena is the perfect age to be going to youth groups."

"Youth groups?" said Rosemary. "Like children's Sunday school?"

"Oh no. They're for teenagers," said Mariana. "They have them at our church. You know, to help the young people to mingle so they can find nice acquaintances."

"Nice Christian acquaintances, you mean?" said Rosemary.

Her mother smiled, saccharine sweet. "Of course."

"Now don't discriminate, Rosemary," said her father. "You know it's illegal to discriminate based on religion."

"I'm not," said Rosemary, furrowing her eyebrows. "I was just clarifying. Besides, people are allowed to have *different* beliefs. That's a human right as well."

Gerald sighed. "We know that all too well from our missionary work."

"That's right," said Mariana. "Why just recently we were in Haiti for several months only. So many of the natives–"

"I don't think that's what you're supposed to call them," said Athena, smiling awkwardly.

"Whoa there, missy," said Gerald with a cheeky grin.

Athena shot her Rosemary an uncomfortable glance.

"Anyway," Mariana continued. "Some of the locals practice hideous witchcraft."

"Totally," said Gerald. "Even worse than my poor dear mother and her fixation with silly fairy tales and herbs and like."

"Oh, boy, do we have a surprise for you," said Rosemary, crossing her arms.

"What was that dear?" Gerald asked.

Athena shook her head vigorously.

"Never mind," said Rosemary, deciding a change of subject was in order. She'd had such little contact with her parents since leaving home, only sending them the briefest of updates about her life. She wasn't entirely sure how to interact with them. "So you've come to visit us?"

"We thought it would be lovely to come and see you after all this time to see how you're settling in. Have you met any nice men here?" Mariana asked.

"Of course," said Rosemary. "There are plenty of nice men around. I've got men coming out my ears."

Her mother shot her a judgmental glance.

Athena looked mortified as she passed her mother a cup of tea.

Rosemary shrugged. "Not in that way."

"What I mean is..." said Mariana, "are you seeing anyone?"

"That's none of your business!" Rosemary protested.

"Of course it is," said Gerald. "You're our daughter. We want you to be happy and to go to heaven."

"And you know that married people go to heaven, is that it?" said Rosemary.

"Well, Rosemary, your upbringing should have taught you

better than this. You know coitus is forbidden outside of marriage."

Rosemary spluttered on her tea. "Don't worry," she said to her parents. "I haven't been doing any of that."

Athena laughed. "How long are you planning on staying?"

Rosemary shot her daughter a grateful glance, relieved to have another change of subject.

"We thought just a few weeks would be ideal," said Mariana. "We wouldn't want to outstay our welcome."

"A few weeks!" said Rosemary.

"Or perhaps longer," said Gerald. "It's been such a long time and we want to spend quality time with you. You know, see if we can help."

"Help with what?" Athena asked, almost gleefully.

"Help to nudge things back on track," said Mariana.

"Things are perfectly fine with the track that they're currently on," Rosemary insisted.

"Glad to hear it, my dear," said Gerald, taking a sip of tea which he'd added rather a lot of milk and sugar to, as was his custom.

Mariana smiled. "Then perhaps we won't need to stay all that long."

Athena beamed at her mother and then turned her attention back to her grandparents. "Are you saying that if you're convinced that we're on track for heaven, you'll move on?"

Gerald's laughter boomed around the room. "She's a funny one, she is!"

"But that's about the size of it," said Mariana. "I mean, if we're not needed we'll go somewhere else where we are. We have a strong calling to do the Lord's work. You understand, don't you?"

"I guess," said Athena.

Gerald looked taken aback by Athena's lukewarm tone. "Don't you feel passionate about something in your life dear?" he asked gently.

Rosemary shot her daughter a warning glance, worried she might mention one of the many things that would encourage her parents to stay for much longer.

"One or two things," said Athena with a slight smile.

Gerald smiled kindly. "Then you must understand that what Mariana and I are passionate about is making sure that our Lord's work is being done here on Earth."

"Alright then," said Rosemary. "Well, I assume you won't need to stay long. We're totally fine. But I suppose we'll find you somewhere to sleep for your short visit. And don't worry. I mean, if the world ends or we die or anything, I'm sure we've got a lot going for us. You could maybe even leave tomorrow."

Mariana laughed. "Oh, don't be silly, dear. We do want to spend quality time with you and make sure things are *really* on track."

Rosemary sighed. "Come on, Athena. Let's get their bags and find them a room."

"You know, this big old house..." said Gerald. "You don't really need all this space. It would make a great facility for a church or maybe even a Bible school."

Rosemary coughed and bit back a retort that would almost certainly have her parents moving in permanently. "Okay, Dad. I'll keep that in mind."

She and Athena found one of the downstairs rooms off the nursery for their uninvited guests to stay.

"All these little beds here," said Mariana. "Who are they for?"

"We had some children visit for a while," said Rosemary. "Err...lost souls, really." She was unsure how else to explain it.

"Helping the unfortunate is all part of God's plan for you," said Mariana with a smile.

"Yeah. Thanks," said Rosemary. "I do feel I've been doing rather a lot of that lately."

She wasn't lying, at least with that comment, though there was certainly a lot of information she was deliberately withholding.

Rosemary left her parents to settle into their room and pulled Athena back to the kitchen.

"What are we going to do?"

"I don't know, they're your parents," said Athena. "Besides, they're not too bad apart from all the slightly over the top religious stuff."

Rosemary sighed. "I suppose I'm still bitter – not just about all the dogma they shoved down my throat as a child, but also about how judgmental they were when I first moved in with Dain. They were even worse when we had you, out of wedlock. Of course they forgave me because of their religious beliefs too. But that didn't make it much better. I can't help but feel they are only being nice because of their beliefs not because it's genuine – and I can never be my true self around them. I don't know how long I can handle this."

"We could just go on holiday," said Athena hopefully.

"What and miss Neve and Nesta's wedding this weekend? I mean, it's tempting to run away, but we can't."

Athena groaned. "I forgot about that. Now I feel like a terrible friend, too."

Rosemary smiled sympathetically. "Don't worry. They've been so busy with the wedding they won't realise about you forgetting. I've hardly even had time to ask Neve about those mysterious people who washed up after the festival. I'm still suspicious of them."

Athena stretched her arms up and scrunched up her face. "Aren't they in a coma?"

"Supposedly," said Rosemary. "But that could be a front."

"Don't you think it's time you went to see a shrink about your paranoia?"

Rosemary glared at her daughter.

"I guess you're right," said Athena. "Not about the people, but about the other thing. We can't go away on holiday yet. We've got to stick around for at least a little while."

"And I need to make sure the chocolate shop is running smoothly," said Rosemary. "How are you feeling, anyway? Any better today with the necklace?"

"Actually, it has been," said Athena. "I feel like I'm getting things under control. But I haven't dared to go outside yet, in case I meet an attractive stranger."

"Well, that's something," said Rosemary. "Oh, and our dastardly cousin paid us a visit at the shop."

"Elamina?"

"Yes."

"What does she want?"

"She's beside herself that I won't take up the invitation to Bermuda. And she warned me that I might be kidnapped or something."

"Err," said Athena. "Maybe you were right to refuse in the first place."

"My thinking exactly," said Rosemary.

"Do you think she's behind all that Bermuda summons stuff?"

"No, she insists she'd rather not have anything to do with me at all. And I can easily believe that she wouldn't want me involved in Bermuda, but maybe it's a trap."

"Why would she want to trap you?" Athena asked. "If she doesn't want anything to do with you?"

"Maybe she wants to steal my magic," Rosemary suggested.

Athena laughed. "Don't be paranoid. She's got plenty of her own magic. Besides the last time you suspected Elamina you were wrong and it was terribly embarrassing, remember?"

"I suppose you're right. Oh, well. I better go whip up a good meal, like a nice roast or something, since it looks like we're having a family dinner tonight."

"Like the good Christian woman you are," said Athena cheekily.

Fourteen

Rosemary was not in the best mood the next morning at the shop. Athena had readily agreed to come in to help, which was just as well as it was Papa Jack's day off and Rosemary wanted the ability to hide in the kitchen if the customers were getting to be too much for her.

"Your window display is excellent, Mum," Athena said admiringly.

"You don't need to cheer me up," said Rosemary, passing her an apron. "I'm fine."

"No, you're not, and besides, I was just being honest. It's amazing you made all those little chocolate sheaths of wheat and everything! I didn't think you knew anything about Lughnasa."

"I don't really," Rosemary admitted, allowing a small smile in appreciation of her daughter's praise. "I just looked it up online and came up with some ideas, but I did enjoy making all those harvest-themed chocolates. I've always loved that kind of thing."

"It's nice to see you in your element," said Athena warmly.

Rosemary smiled again, wider this time. "It would actually be helpful to know more about the festival. I'm not sure if it will be a problem or not, but it's better to be prepared."

Athena shrugged. "It's the beginning of the harvest – you know, harvests were a really big deal in the old days. Ferg will be busy baking special loaves of bread and stuff now, but traditionally, they had to wait for the festival day to start eating the new grain crops of the season, so it was a pretty big deal."

Rosemary's mind flicked back to the wheatfield that Burk brought her to on their date, wondering how many harvest traditions he had witnessed over the centuries. The image of the dying vampire woman stuck in her mind's eye, with the purple feather in her chest, lying there before bursting into dust.

"It's named after the sun god, Lugh," Athena continued. "But you probably already worked that one out."

Rosemary nodded as she finished setting out the bonbons and truffles. "Sun god, sure. Sounds important."

"Of course he is," said Athena. "After all, the sun brings life and everything. Lugh is an important deity and so is Rosemerta."

"Who's that?"

"She's a harvest goddess. You know, she'd look at home in the middle of your window display with all the grains and bread. Sometimes she's considered Lugh's wife, though I'm not sure how matrimony works for gods. They're rather mysterious."

"Mysterious and enormous," Rosemary agreed. "I doubt they care about witch politics."

Athena raised her eyebrows curiously.

"Never mind."

Rosemary busied herself with preparing some new hazelnut creams with a glamour charm designed to make people feel more confident and sophisticated, and therefore look that way. The recipe wasn't working too well, so she gave up and slumped over the counter instead, trying to work out how to resolve her parental problems.

An hour later, Marjie entered the chocolate shop, carrying a plate of scones and another of pasties. "I've brought you some lunch." She caught sight of Rosemary's face. "Oh deary me. Why so glum?"

"Have you ever had the misfortune of meeting Gerald Thorn?"

Marjie laughed. "Oh dear, let me guess, your ma and pa are visiting?"

Athena nodded, but Rosemary only grimaced.

"They're really not that bad, Mum."

Rosemary narrowed her eyes. "If that's true, why are you here helping me out and not at home?"

Marjie tutted. "That Gerald always was odd duck."

"I'm dying to find out why," said Athena. "Mum can't explain to me how a powerful witch like Granny Thorn managed to produce a son like that. Especially growing up in Myrtlewood..."

Marjie chuckled. "You know, even as a child, Gerald was a funny old bean. He had no aptitude for magic, which is probably why Galdie did it."

"Did what?" Rosemary asked, suddenly intrigued.

Normally she tried to think as little about her parents as possible lest she lose the plot completely, but the thought that her father wasn't entirely to blame for the way he'd turned out had never occurred to her.

"She never told me the details," Marjie continued. "But I'd be surprised if she didn't cast memory charms on him – you know – to remove all knowledge of magic."

"How awful," said Athena.

"Well, Granny certainly knew how to mess with people's memories," Rosemary grumbled, pushing down a rising resentment that she'd thought she had already let go of regarding her own mind being muddled.

Marjie sighed. "Well, I'm sure she thought it was for the best. Poor Gerald was miserable as a child. He inherited all the warmth and Ada got the magic, which meant she always had the upper hand."

"So she waved her magic wand and solved everything," said Rosemary darkly.

Athena passed her a lavender rose cream from the cabinet and she gulped it down, allowing the fragrant bonbon to work its magic, calming the nerves and sweetening her mood.

"Oh love," said Marjie. "I'm sure she felt she was protecting her little boy from being left out in a magical town. You see, when he was younger, Galdie fretted about him not being magically-inclined, and later on he seemed to have no idea about the stuff. He just wandered around, mildly baffled all the time. He chose to go away to school, and by then he had fallen in with the wrong crowd – evangelical Methodists, you understand."

"Far too well," Rosemary muttered, though her mood had softened from resentful to slightly sad.

"So he chose a religious school, of course," Marjie continued.

"He never looked back. I often wondered about him. I'm sure Galdie felt guilty about it all."

"That didn't stop her from taking my memories of magic away too."

Marjie absentmindedly popped a chocolate sample from the counter into her mouth and sighed. "Oh, that one's nice. I'll have ten of those."

"Papa Jack's been experimenting," Rosemary explained, gesturing at the sample truffles. "That one's supposed to give you a little boost of excitement, though he suspects it may spice things up in the bedroom too. I should have warned you."

"Better make it twenty then. I'll have a surprise for Herb when he comes home."

Rosemary and Athena both paled and looked at each other.

Marjie cackled. "Anyway. I always thought the reason Gerald turned to religion was to fill a void left by his missing memories."

"That makes sense, in a way," said Athena. "I'm glad you didn't do that, though, Mum. Religion has far too many rules for me!"

Rosemary shook her head sadly. "I feel sorry for him, now."

"Too right," said Marjie. "Besides, all that was before Galdie knew much about fae memory magic, I'd wager. Whatever she did to Gerald, the magic she used would have been older and more crude than what she used on you."

Marjie bade them farewell, smiling as she took the truffles Athena had wrapped up for her.

Athena nibbled on a soothing peppermint crisp. "You know, I'm starting to think Granny Thorn wasn't a great parent."

"You don't say."

Fifteen

Athena tugged down the hem of her gold satin dress as she got out of the car.

"I hope it isn't too short," she said as her mother walked around to meet her.

"It looks great, love," said Rosemary. "And I'm pretty sure that's what counts as a respectable length these days."

Athena shrugged. "Who knows? We're hardly fashion experts."

Rosemary took Athena's arm and began walking her toward the back entrance to Nesta's garden. "It'll be fine," she said. "As far as I know, no fashion police are on the guest list."

Athena laughed.

She noticed the sound of soft violin music as they drew closer. They entered through an archway of roses and looked around at the gorgeous setting.

"Nesta's garden is usually beautiful," said Rosemary, "but this is stunning."

Indeed it was. The natural beauty of the garden was enhanced by the presence of lace in many forms: giant lacy white fans were dotted about, some hung from the trees, as did a number of lace parasols, all giving off a whimsical, old-fashioned vibe. Enchanted white and red butterflies fluttered around in the air. Athena couldn't tell if they were real insects or just an illusion, but either way the effect was stunning.

"Oooh, hammocks!" said Rosemary, eyeing up the many lace hammocks that were strung from the trees. "That's where you'll find me."

"Not yet," said Athena, pulling her mother back. "We need to be polite and say hello first."

Neve was waiting nervously by the back doorstep, all dressed up in a red silk suit.

"You look glamorous!" said Rosemary.

"I suppose I'm the 'husband'," Neve said, with a frown. "Nesta wants to make a grand entrance and I can't be bothered. I still think weddings are a load of patriarchal tosh..."

"But yours is different," said Athena. "So don't go stressing about heteronormative gender roles, just enjoy it."

"Besides, this is rather gorgeous for patriarchal tosh," Rosemary added as they both hugged their friend.

Neve laughed. "I suppose you're right. Nesta has put a lot of work into it. I'd better just appreciate that and do my best to enjoy it."

"That's the spirit," said Rosemary.

"Just think of it as a glamorous party with all your friends," said Athena. "We're all here to celebrate you and Nesta because you're special to us."

Neve smiled warmly. "Thanks," she said.

"Now let me distract you with shop talk," said Rosemary. "You know how I told you about how we found that poor vampire woman in the field. Have you heard anything?"

Neve shook her head. "There was a sighting nearby, that's all I know. A local farmer saw a couple of suspicious people in the next field over, fleeing towards Finn's Creek."

"Did they describe them?"

"Just as a man and a woman, oddly dressed. But don't worry about all that. The vampire authorities are handling it. It's their business, not ours."

Rosemary narrowed her eyes. "A couple, like those people who were found on the beach?"

Neve raised an eyebrow. "You mean the two people who are still in a coma?"

"Supposedly," said Rosemary. "But have you even seen them?"

"No," Neve admitted. "And security is tight, so don't even think about paying them a visit. You'll get me into trouble. I shouldn't have even told you they were there, really, even though you've done some work for us before."

"Of fine." Rosemary mock-pouted, but Athena could tell she was really smiling inside, achieving her other goal of distracting Neve from her wedding jitters with shop talk.

Athena decided to join in. "So is there anything you can tell me about Bermuda and why we're being summoned?"

"Yes," said Rosemary. "I'm sure all these things are somehow connected."

"You really think so?" Neve asked.

"Of course Mum does," said Athena. "She's incredibly paranoid. Now come on, Mum, let's let Neve have a moment of peace."

Neve laughed. "Anything do to with Bermuda is above my pay grade, I'm afraid, but thanks for the chat. I needed that distraction to snap me out of my fretting. I love Nesta so much. I can't help thinking that things are so perfect between us that they're bound to go wrong."

Those words settled heavily on Athena as she recognised her own similar fear. Things had been so good with Elise, but everything else ran the risk of ruining it.

As if in answer to her thoughts she heard a familiar voice. "There you are!"

Elise was approaching in a strappy silver dress.

Athena broke away from Rosemary to hug her girlfriend. "You look gorgeous!" she said.

"So do you!" said Elise. "It looks like we intentionally dressed to match – gold and silver! Only we never talked about our outfits, did we? You were sick..."

"Oh...yes," said Athena. She hadn't seen Elise since the incident in the ice cream parlour.

"I have to admit, I overreacted after you ran away from me the other day. I felt abandoned, but then I realised I was being silly and making it all about me when you were ill. Feeling better?"

"Much," said Athena, feeling her anxiety rising. She really

had to tell Elise what was going on, there was no two ways about it, but she needed to find the right words. "Only, there's something I wanted to tell you about…"

A tinkling bell interrupted.

"Ladies, gentlemen, and other gentle folk!" Ferg bellowed. He was dressed in a lacy white robe, standing on a little platform outlined in an arch covered with roses. "Gather round, dear friends, for the ceremony is about to start."

"Come on," said Elise. "Let's get a good seat. We can talk later."

Athena nodded, her anxiety subsiding, at least for the moment. She followed Elise toward the neat little rows of white seats. They sat down near the front, behind the rows reserved for family, to ensure they had a good view.

"There's Neve," said Elise. "She looks nervous."

Neve stood awkwardly near the front, looking as if she'd rather be pacing around.

"She'll be fine," said Athena. "She's just having a slight freak out and a crisis of values."

Elise shot Athena a worried look.

"But nothing major," Athena reassured her.

Moments later, the seated audience hushed as beautiful slow cello music started up.

They turned their heads to watch as little Mei exited the door of the house, dressed in a red silk suit just like Neve's. She began walking down the aisle between rows of chairs, scattering rose petals out of a wicker basket, followed closely behind by the other foundling children, all clad in a combination of white lace and red silk.

"Don't they look adorable?" Athena whispered. Elise squeezed her arm in response.

The music changed to a grander-sounding tune and Nesta appeared, resplendent in a flowing white lace dress and a hooded cloak of red silk. She carried a bouquet of red and white roses.

"The queen of hearts," Athena whispered.

"Of all our hearts," Elise added, and indeed, Nesta held a special place in many people's hearts, as did Neve.

Athena took Elise's hand as the ceremony began, trying not to giggle at Ferg's elaborate gesticulating.

The whole audience sighed in delight multiple times as Neve and Nesta exchanged very sweet and personal vows.

Elise and Athena watched, transfixed, as the brides held up their right hands, interlacing their fingers while Ferg wrapped a red ribbon around and around them, symbolising the handfasting, the formal joining of their lives in the ancient pagan tradition.

Athena squeezed Elise's hand, wondering if they too could have something like this one day, but her overthinking mind got the better of her. She and Elise were too young, after all. They were bound to mess things up before they could reach this kind of milestone. Athena felt a pang of guilt over what she still hadn't told Elise.

Ferg held up his hands dramatically.

"As this knot is tied, so are your lives bound.

Woven into this cord, imbued into its very fiery fibres, are your hopes and the hopes of your friends and family, for your life together.

With the fashioning of this knot I tie the desires, dreams, love, and happiness wished here in this place to your lives for as long as love shall last.

May it be granted that what is done before the gods be not undone by man.

Two entwined in love, bound by commitment and fear, sadness and joy, by hardship and victory, anger and reconciliation, all of which brings strength to this union.

Hold tight to one another through both good times and bad, and watch as your strength grows.

So mote it be!"

The crowd cheered and rose from their seats, and rose petals rained down magically from the sky, mingling with the butterflies dancing in the air. Athena thought she recognised the magical signature of the charm, and she glanced towards Marjie, who winked.

"Now, you wanted to talk about something?" said Elise as the gathered crowd began to make their way towards the newlyweds.

"Oh...yes," Athena said, and then her heart caught in her throat. She was terrified of ruining things with Elise and needed more time to think about what to say. "Uhh. Let's...let's just go and congratulate Neve and Nesta first."

They wandered up the aisle. Rosemary walked past them, saying, "If you need me, I'll be in a hammock being fed canapes and champagne by the catering staff."

"Your mum sure knows how to have a good time," said Elise, grinning.

Athena laughed. "I'm glad she's enjoying herself and relaxing for a change."

They approached Neve and Nesta.

"That was beautiful!" said Elise. "I almost cried."

Neve laughed. "Well, my aunt and parents in the front row were bawling their eyes out," she said.

"Thank you both for coming," said Nesta, giving Elise and Athena a double hug.

"It was really special," said Athena. "I wouldn't have missed it for the world."

"Oh!" said Nesta. "The music's starting up!"

And indeed, the familiar sound of Celtic guitar was drifting across the garden.

"Come on, my love," Nesta said to Neve. "We've got to have our first dance!"

Neve looked mildly mortified.

Elise and Athena giggled as they followed towards the clearing set aside for dancing, dodging out of Marjie's way as the older woman waved her hands with a flourish, magically rearranging the ceremony seating into table-settings for the meal ahead.

"It's so romantic," said Elise, watching the bridal pair begin to dance slowly across the lawn.

Athena began to agree, but realised she'd started feeling odd. Her heart thudded in her chest. "Umm," she said. "I wanted to say…"

"Shh," said Elise. "After the dancing."

Athena sighed and looked around for the source of the music. Sure enough, between some of the gathering crowd, she recognised a familiar face.

The travelling minstrel from the pub was seated, with his guitar and green waistcoat. He looked up and across, directly at Athena, and her she felt a tingling sensation, followed by a jaunty urge to dance.

It seemed the whole crowd felt the same, for as the music picked up, everyone took to the dance floor. Elise and Athena danced together, though Athena couldn't help but shoot glances at the minstrel. She intended to be suspicious of him, but her doubts quickly faded into something else entirely.

"He's great, isn't he?" said Elise. "Is that the musician from the pub that everyone keeps talking about?"

Athena nodded, and then was quickly swept up in the spirit of the dancing. On and on it went, with various folk-dances initiated while everyone joined in. Well, almost everyone; Athena saw no sign of her mother and suspected the hammocks were proving too relaxing to leave. Athena was almost too swept up in the joy of dancing to notice, anyway. She felt free and glorious as she spun around, her arms in the air.

As the music wound down, she felt another sensation growing, a mesmerising pull.

"Just a quick break for dinner, folks," said the travelling minstrel. "Then I'll be back with you afterwards."

Athena felt as if she was in a dream, pulled against the tide of people who were heading towards dinner, and she made her way towards the minstrel.

"Hello," he said, standing up with a twinkle in his eye. "And you are?"

"Athena," she replied. She couldn't help staring at his handsome face.

"I'm Cailean O'Donohue," he replied, maintaining eye contact as he held out his hand to Athena.

She reached out to shake, but instead found that he'd lifted if to his lips to kiss her knuckles. Athena felt her insides melt. *Could it be that I love this man…Cailean O'Donoghue?"*

The world seemed to fade away around them and she found herself pulled into his arms and into a passionate kiss.

"Athena!"

Athena pulled back at the yell, turning to see Elise's shocked face.

"What?" Athena said, coming to her senses and suddenly being slammed with embarrassment and shame.

What have I done?

Elise turned and ran away.

Athena followed after her.

"Leave me alone," Elise said when Athena reached her in a quiet corner of the garden.

"I'm sorry," said Athena. "I was trying to tell you."

"Trying to tell me what? That you've been cheating on me with a travelling minstrel?!"

"No," said Athena. "It's way more complicated than that." She sighed.

Hearing the sadness in Athena's voice, Elise seemed to soften. "Then tell me," she said more gently. "What in Brigid's name is going on with you?"

"It's...I don't know how to explain," said Athena.

"Then don't bother," said Elise, angrily beginning to storm off again.

Athena reached out to stop her. "No, wait," she said. "It's just something that happens."

Elise gave her a pointed look. "*That's* your grand explanation?"

"No, please let me finish," said Athena. "It's a coming of age...erm...symptom. Dad said it happens to the high fae. They get this stupid infatuation thing where they suddenly fall for people...random strangers. It's awful, really!"

Elise folded her arms.

"So you're saying you're entrapped by fae magic? Your own fae magic?"

Athena nodded. "Dad says it's just a temporary thing, that it will wear off, at least from my side of things."

"You mean even once it wears off, people will still be all over you?" Elise asked.

"There are ways to get it under control, more or less," said Athena. "I can channel the magic into creative pursuits or learn how mute it myself."

Elise sighed. "That does sound kind of awful," she admitted. "I'm sorry you have to go through it."

"It is awful," said Athena. "I hate losing control of myself, of my body. I was scared of telling you."

"But you were trying to tell me before?"

Athena nodded.

Elise frowned. "This is what was affecting you at the ice cream parlour, isn't it?"

"Yes," said Athena. "That was when it was first starting, I think."

"Why didn't you tell me earlier?" Elise sounded frustrated. "Why wait until the wedding and ruin a wonderful night?"

"I'm sorry," said Athena again. "I was trying to figure out what it was. Dad didn't think to mention it earlier, and we had no clue what was happening. I thought it might have been some kind of spell."

"Is that really the reason?" Elise asked.

Athena hung her head. "Part of it," she admitted. "I was also scared of how you'd react, scared of losing you..."

Elise sighed. "I wish you wouldn't keep things from me; you know I hate that. And how long is all this supposed to go on for?"

Athena let out a long, slow breath. "A couple of months, maybe."

"Months!"

"That's exactly how I reacted," said Athena, "but I'm going to get it under control. I've got Mum's special necklace, see." She gestured to the emerald pendant. "I think it's helping a bit. I feel a lot less woozy anyway, and I've been painting..."

"Painting?" Elise raised her eyebrows in surprise.

"Yes, anything is worth a try. Dad thinks creative outlets will reduce the problem and I think it's all helping...except..."

"Except for when you get swept away by attractive minstrels?"

"I suppose..." said Athena, with a sinking feeling that all hope was lost. "I'm sorry."

"No, I'm sorry," said Elise, in a quiet voice. "I don't think I can do this..."

"Elise." Athena's heart wrenched. "Please...I can't lose you."

"And I can't just sit around biding my time while my girl-friend falls in love with random strangers!" said Elise. "I love you, Athena, I do, but think about it from my perspective..."

Athena felt herself deflate. "You're right. You don't deserve this."

"Maybe we just need to take a little break while you figure this out," said Elise gently.

"I suppose that's wise," said Athena. "I really don't want to hurt you any more than I already have."

Elise gave her a sad smile. "And I wish I could help you get through this," she said. "But I think it's one of those things you're just going to have to face alone."

"And hopefully, you'll still be here when this is all over..."

"Hopefully..."

Athena watched Elise walk away, feeling her eyes burn as the tears began running down her cheeks. She turned towards the hammocks, walking as if in a sad trance. The pain in her chest was so intense she wondered whether she needed a doctor.

"There you are," said Rosemary's voice from one of the hanging lacy bundles. "Ready for dinner? Oh—what is it, love?"

Athena sobbed and wiped at the tears. "It was awful, Mum."

Her mother rose from the hammock and wrapped Athena in a big hug as she continued to sob. "I tried—to tell—Elise," Athena said, between sobs. "But there was no—chance. And then—I kissed—the minstrel."

"You what?"

"It was the fae—magic thing," said Athena. "And then—Elise broke up with me."

"Oh no," said Rosemary. "Did you explain?"

"Yes," said Athena. "But she says—she says she can't do it. She can't sit around while I become—infatuated with—random strangers."

Rosemary sighed. "I'm so sorry, love."

"It hurts."

"Of course it does," said Rosemary. "It's your first break-up. Your heart's broken."

"That's why they call it that," said Athena. "I never understood before...It really does feel like my heart is breaking open in my chest."

She collapsed further into her mother's arms as Rosemary intensified her hug.

"I don't know how I'll live with this," said Athena. "How can I even survive this much pain?"

"It will fade," Rosemary promised. "Slowly."

Athena's sobs intensified again, but she was too upset to even care about embarrassment.

"Maybe we need a little change of scenery, after all," said Rosemary.

"What are you talking about?" Athena asked.

"Well, I've been reconsidering the invitation to Bermuda while relaxing in the hammock. It really does make sense to go willingly rather than being 'detained', doesn't it? And maybe it will be a nice tropical holiday and keep you distracted by the magical bureaucracy. Plus, if there's a chance of some kind of magical peace talks, then I suppose it's in my interests for them to succeed."

"Being a million miles from here does sound like a good idea about now," said Athena. "When can we leave?"

"I'll find out," said Rosemary. "But if Papa Jack is happy minding the shop, perhaps we can go in a few days and stay away for a couple of weeks."

"We'll miss the Lughnasa ritual," said Athena.

"You know," said Rosemary, "I was counting that as a bonus. The rituals seem to attract magical mayhem and we've had quite enough of that already!"

"And what about your parents?"

"An extra bonus!"

"Mum, isn't it unfair abandoning them like that?" Athena folded her arms and frowned. "As much as I want to."

"Not in the slightest," said Rosemary. "They don't think twice about skipping the country for their religious pursuits, and besides, they'll be off as soon as they decide there are more worthy souls to save elsewhere. To be quite frank, I'd rather not waste their time. My soul has never been happier than it is being a witch in Myrtlewood!"

Sixteen

Two days later, Rosemary and Athena trundled their suitcases along the polyester diamond-patterned carpet, looking for the signs for the right gate to board the plane to Bermuda.

"This is heavy," said Athena. "I told you we should have taken them up on the offer of magical transportation. I bet Dad and Burk did that. It sounds so cool!"

"I told you the teleport thing that Juniper does made me feel terribly ill and that was just a short distance. I'd hate to think what it would be like going all the way to the tropics."

"I suppose that letter they sent did have a list of potential side effects and recovery times," said Athena. "But I'm sure it'd be less of a hassle than having to go on such a long flight with a transfer in Dubai."

"Oh, it'll be fun," said Rosemary. "You've never been on a long flight before. You've barely been on any flights."

"That's true. I'm just used to the magical way of doing things now. Everything is so much more efficient. How do you think Dad and Burk are finding it over in Bermuda?"

"I haven't heard anything," said Rosemary. "I wonder if their cell phones even work over there. But don't worry, we'll soon find out what it's like."

"I'm surprised they were able to arrange such last minute flights, but it's funny how you couldn't wait to get out of the house as soon as your parents arrived."

"Do you blame me?" Rosemary asked. "Look, here's the right gate. Twenty minutes until boarding. I might go get a cup of tea or even a coffee."

"Coffee?!" Athena's eyes widened.

"It's what you're supposed to drink at airports, isn't it?"

Athena smiled at her mother. "I'll have a cappuccino. Wait a minute—"

"What?"

Athena pointed to the screen at the top of the gate. "It says the flight to Bermuda has been cancelled."

Rosemary looked up to see the red flashing words next to their flight number. "Oh bother!"

They made their way over to the information desk only to discover there were no more available flights to Bermuda that day or the following day either.

"We can put you on the next one," said the woman. "It'll be Wednesday."

Rosemary sighed. "I suppose I can deal with my parents until then."

The woman gave her a sympathetic look.

"Airports really take it out of you, don't they?" she said as they pulled up outside Thorn Manor. "I'm exhausted. And here I was, finally raring to go on this ridiculous trip. At least my parents will be gone by now. It's just kind of disappointing not to be in a tropical paradise. "

"Don't worry," said Athena. "We'll be able to go in a couple more days."

However, as they reached the front door of their home, a familiar looking scroll with a red seal was pinned to it.

Rosemary picked it up cautiously.

"What does it say?" Athena asked, reaching for the parchment.

"Our presence is no longer required," said Rosemary, passing it over.

"What does that mean?"

"It means they've rescinded the invitation to Bermuda. Just when I was getting used to the idea." She sighed. *So much for spending more time with a certain handsome vampire.*

Athena groaned in disappointment.

The door opened and Rosemary's parents appeared, dressed in matching orange parkas.

"You're back!" they both said simultaneously.

"I'm afraid so," said Rosemary, smiling.

"Things didn't go well with the flight then?" Gerald said.

"No," Rosemary. "I thought you were leaving since we weren't going to be here."

"Well, we did think we'd leave, originally," said Mariana. "But then we thought Myrtlewood could do with a little Christian cheer."

"We can't even find a church in town. Can you believe it?" said Gerald. "We thought we might start a little group. You know, knock on the doors and see who else is interested in the teachings of the Lord."

Rosemary stifled a sigh. "You're kidding?"

"Dead serious," said Gerald. "You can come with us if you like."

Rosemary and Athena gave each other a look.

"I think we're a little bit tired today," Athena muttered.

"Exhausted," said Rosemary.

"Maybe tomorrow then," said Mariana.

They watched as Rosemary's parents wandered down the driveway.

Athena shook her head. "Going door knocking." She visibly cringed.

"And worst of all, they're still here." Rosemary felt helpless as she dragged her bags inside.

"To think we could be relaxing in the tropics now."

Rosemary collapsed onto the window seats. "Don't remind me."

Seventeen

Athena had woken from a nap after the airport debacle feeling slightly strange. Her first instinct was to do some more painting.

Overall, she'd been holding up well. She hadn't had any strange experiences in the airport despite the crowds of strangers.

Between her creative outlet and the emerald pendant, she felt almost normal, except that her heart ached, missing Elise.

Athena was determined to do whatever she could to prove herself, to show that she was in control, to show Elise she was worth being with – that it wasn't too much of a risk.

She still felt acute pain in her chest every time she thought of the blue haired girl she'd fallen for. But she was also relieved for the space to figure things out on her own without constantly having to try to convince anyone things were okay.

There was a soft tapping sound from the French doors that lead to Athena's balcony. She opened the blinds to see Finnigan.

"What are you doing here?"

He smiled. "Just paying a visit." He brushed the hair out of his eyes. "I wanted to see you."

"Get out. You're not invited, in case you didn't already know."

Finnigan's smile widened. "I have a message for you."

Athena frowned. "What is it?"

"Open the doors."

Athena hesitated but didn't want to appear scared, so she opened the doors and then put her hands on her hips. "All right. Tell me the message and then leave."

"This," he said, producing a bright purple feather. "This is for your mother."

He waved it around in the air and then handed it to Athena, looking her in the eye. Athena stared back at him, anger burning in her chest.

"That's the message?" she asked.

Finnigan gazed at her. "No. The message is for you both. Stay out of things that you don't understand."

Athena felt a prickle of fear chill her spine.

"More cryptic messages?"

He shrugged.

"You can leave now." She began shutting the door.

"Wait," said Finnigan putting his hand up to block her.

"What?"

"There's something different about you." He was staring at Athena.

"Well...the theory is—"

"You're coming of age!" said Finnigan, his eyes lighting up.

"Isn't it wonderful?"

Athena wanted to yell at him to go away, but as she looked at him, her gaze lingered on his eyes. Her anger dissolved as a wave of attraction overwhelmed her.

She tried to resist it.

Finnigan stepped closer, smiling that charming smile, touching a hand her cheek.

"Athena...isn't it wonderful? Don't fight it. Accept who you are."

"Stop it," said Athena, but her voice was muted just as much as her anger was. She was submerged in too many confusing feelings – feelings for Finnigan, old emotions being re-awakened, and new possibilities emerging along with them.

"You've always been special, Athena," Finnigan said. "Special to me..."

Athena felt a swooning sensation in her abdomen. She reached out for him. But then a jolt of hot anger burned up to her throat from wherever it had been contained within her.

White light blasted out, knocking him back to the end of the balcony onto his arse.

"Get out," she said. "Don't come here again."

She closed the French doors and locked them, drawing the curtains, then she dove into her bed, still feeling the confusing emotions circling in her mind.

Do I really still have feelings for Finnigan? Or is it just the awakening of my fae magic? Could it be both?

She hoped it was nothing and that it would fade, but unlike the other experiences of her coming-of-age inspired infatuation, the feelings for Finnigan seemed to linger.

"Curse that bastard," Athena muttered into her pillow. "I hope I never have to see him again."

Eighteen

Rosemary arrived at the shop the next day feeling somewhat deflated. It turned out she'd become rather attached to the idea of going to Bermuda, after all. Going back to her regular life, as delightful as it might be, didn't seem quite right, at least not at that moment.

The day dragged on and Rosemary became more and more exhausted. She felt even worse when she arrived back at Thorn Manor that evening to find her parents had taken over the lounge with group of polyester wearing strangers. It was a Bible study group with a handful of apparently interested local Christians they'd picked up from door knocking every house in Myrtlewood.

"Don't mind us, dear," said Gerald. "We'll be a few more hours yet."

"Great," said Rosemary.

"I tried to stop them," Athena said, coming downstairs. "But they were very insistent."

"I bet they were," said Rosemary. "So what should we have for dinner?"

"No idea. I was hoping you would have brought something back from Marjie's."

"I'm afraid not today. We'll have to cook or maybe have beans on toast."

Just then, the doorbell rang. They answered it to find Reginald Orthorne standing there on the doorstep looking red faced and frustrated.

"What is the meaning of this?" he blustered.

"What do you mean?" Rosemary asked.

"You were expected in Bermuda yesterday!"

"Our flights were cancelled," said Athena.

"And then we were told not to come," Rosemary added.

"Excuses, excuses."

"Seriously?" said Athena. "Are you saying we *are* still invited?"

"Of course you are. We're expecting you to arrive at the airport, but you weren't on the plane."

"You're saying the flight wasn't actually cancelled?" Rosemary asked.

"Stop with this nonsense," said Reginald. "You have five minutes."

"Excuse me?" Rosemary raised her eyebrows.

"Go and pack your bags," Reginald instructed. "The Arch Magistrate is enraged."

"Fine, we'll go," said Rosemary. "But we're going to need longer than five minutes to pack."

Reginald pulled a small pocket watch out of his wallet. "Alright, twenty-five minutes."

"I'm not a child," Rosemary protested.

"Go!" said Reginald.

Rosemary and Athena clumped upstairs to repack the bags. They returned a short time later and told Rosemary's parents they were about to go to Bermuda after all.

"Do you need lift to the airport?" Mariana asked.

"No," said Rosemary. "I think we'll be fine."

She made her way back out to the front of the house and closed the front door behind her and Athena.

"Right. How does this go then?" Athena asked.

Reginald took hold of both of their wrists. "Hold on tight to your luggage and close your eyes."

They followed his instructions.

Rosemary immediately felt the familiar swirling, nauseating sensation that she'd experienced when Juniper had teleported her previously, only this time, it was heavier, felt much worse, and went on for a lot longer.

There was darkness, only darkness. Rosemary wondered what kind of hellscape they'd been transported to.

Nineteen

"Your senses will return to normal in five minutes," said Reginald's disembodied voice. "And I'm afraid you'll feel off for some time, possibly a few hours. But you can relax until you've recovered. You're safe in your rooms. Someone will call on you later in the day to let you know of the proceedings."

Rosemary couldn't even reply. She had no voice and could see nothing other than darkness, but gradually she came to her senses and looked around.

Athena was already up looking out the window as Rosemary pulled herself to a sitting position.

"Oh my gosh, Mum. Look, it's beautiful!"

"Don't you feel ill?" Rosemary asked.

"A little, but it's wearing off."

Rosemary groaned. "I'm glad one of us is feeling alright."

Athena helped her to a chair where she collapsed. Moments

later, Rosemary felt a cold damp facecloth that Athena placed over her eyes.

She fell into a light nap. By the time she woke up she did feel a lot better.

Rosemary looked around, blinking into the light as she stretched, still sitting in the same armchair.

"This place is brilliant," said Athena. "Aren't you glad we came?"

"Not exactly," said Rosemary. "All I've seen is the inside of a hotel room."

"It's a nice room, though. Isn't it?"

Rosemary took a closer look around the suite. It was indeed quite luxurious and not too over the top. Some tasteful and modern witch had clearly done the decorating rather than someone with Elamina's gaudy sense of style.

"It is nice," said Rosemary. "I can see the appeal."

She got up from the chair feeling only slightly woozy and crossed to the window. The immaculate view looked out on miles of aquamarine Atlantic Ocean and a clear horizon.

"It's a beautiful day," said Athena. "Maybe this will be just the holiday we need."

Rosemary smiled and put her arm around her daughter. "I do very much hope that you're right."

There was a knock at the door. Athena opened it to find Dain and Burk both standing there. She waved them inside.

"You made it," said Burk, approaching Rosemary and pulling her into an uncharacteristically public display of affection.

Rosemary pulled away from him and looked around to find

that Athena and Dain were staring out the window, studiously ignoring them.

"How was the trip?" Burk asked.

"Well, it was awful," said Rosemary. "But it was all over pretty quickly."

Burk nodded.

"Any idea what's going on here?" Rosemary asked.

"They haven't told us yet," Dain said. "Apparently we're supposed to take some time to adjust, you know...enjoy the resort vibes and settle in."

"Sounds like a great idea," said Athena. "You've been here for a few days. Show us around, will you? I want a drink with a little umbrella."

They spent the rest of the day relaxing in the tropical paradise. Rosemary was astonished to find that the bathrooms were all coral pink, lined with elegant tiles complete with fountains, and young pasty-skinned bathroom attendants who offered to help wash the hands of everyone who entered. It was all a little bit much, and Rosemary hoped they were well paid considering their awkward employment.

She got a much needed massage at the magical spa downstairs, while Athena lounged by the pool with Dain. Burk, not much one for sunlight, said he had other matters to attend to but gave Rosemary his spare room key in case she wanted to visit later.

She smiled, feeling like she was enjoying herself more and more.

That evening she considered going to visit Burk before dinner. While comparing outfits in her room there was a knock at the door. A tall man clad in a black suit with salt and pepper hair and matching bushy moustache informed her she was being summoned by the Arch Magistrate.

Rosemary gaped. She clutched at her wrists with a twinge of vulnerability. Athena was down in the restaurant having dinner with Dain. Perhaps that was a good thing. Rosemary was unsure if the situation might put her in undue danger.

She followed the man down the hall and then down another hall and another. The walls around her turned from the plain light modern hotel room decor into what appeared to be more like an ancient castle with torches on the walls and everything.

Rosemary made a note to bring Athena down to show her later. However, it turned out there was no need.

Grand golden engraved doors opened and she wandered in to a huge high-ceilinged hall. Elevated seating surrounded her on both sides, full of unfamiliar faces.

As she walked forwards all heads turned towards her. Rosemary realised she was being stared at by fancy witch representatives from all around the world. Many of them wore robes and ornate clothing that Rosemary assumed was particular to whichever country they came from. They all sat in comfortable-looking velvet chairs.

Up ahead was a fancy elevated platform, golden and engraved with mythological patterns. It was complete with a seat that looked like a throne, which Rosemary assumed was for the Arch Magistrate.

Despite Elamina implying the official leader of the witching world was a woman, Rosemary hadn't been able to shake her expectations of a wizardly figure with a long white beard.

She was surprised instead to find a rather petite, librarian-looking figure with walnut-coloured skin and a black bob streaked with silver. She was wearing an emerald green skirt-suit and horn rimmed spectacles.

"Madame Thorn," she said in a confident, throaty voice. "You've finally made it."

Rosemary looked around and noticed Athena, Dain, and Burk standing up the front along with a handful of other people.

"Erm, Madame Thorn was my grandmother. I'm just Rosemary."

The Arch Magistrate raised her eyebrows and there was a murmur through the crowd.

"What's going on?" Rosemary whispered to Athena as she came to stand next to her.

"We're about to find out," Athena replied.

"Thank you all for joining us," said the Arch Magistrate, standing up from her throne on her sensible black heels. "I suppose you're wondering why you've been summoned."

"You can say that again," said Rosemary quietly.

Athena elbowed her.

"It has come to my attention recently," the magistrate continued, "that there are new opportunities for peace. For many years, vampires, witches, druids, and fae have largely kept to themselves. When we weren't at war, that is. There have been significant tensions over the years when we've mixed."

She gave Burk and Rosemary a long glance.

Rosemary's gut tightened. She was vaguely aware that vampire-witch relationships used to be forbidden a long time ago and wasn't sure if the witching parliament, as archaic as it looked, had caught up to the times.

"However," the Arch Magistrate continued, "times are changing and modern times call for modern measures." Rosemary felt her shoulders relax. "We propose a peace treaty."

There was a hum of voices around the hall. Some sounded pleased, while others did not.

"Okay," said Rosemary. "So why are we here, exactly?"

Athena elbowed her again.

The Arch Magistrate gave her a patient look, like a school teacher addressing a small child. "You have been identified as either key messengers or those who may hold useful diplomatic roles, because of your...characteristics and relationships."

Rosemary pondered this for a moment. Dain and Athena were fae, and not just any fae. They were fae royalty, apparently, although she didn't know much about it. Dain had left the fae realm so young and Athena had only been there fleetingly.

She and Athena were also witches, and not just any witches – they were powerful Thorn witches. Not to mention Rosemary's close connections with a certain vampire who apparently had been summoned as a sort of emissary for his kind.

She wasn't sure who the other oddly dressed beings standing next to them were. Most were clad in robes just like many of the seated parliamentary witches were. Rosemary felt under-dressed. She assumed the others gathered next to her shared some similarly "useful" qualities, but the whole situation still seemed ridiculous.

"Why did you call us all the way here to ask us about this?"

Rosemary asked. "Why not just pop over for a cup of tea sometime?"

There was silence in the room. Rosemary caught sight of her cousin Elamina sitting on the back benches, looking pale and clearly hoping nobody remembered the family connection.

Rosemary felt her shoulders tightening. She'd clearly said the wrong thing and she hoped that didn't mean she'd be thrown into the dungeons, because this place certainly looked like it would have proper dungeons. That was the moment she realised she'd been speaking all her thoughts aloud and Athena's face was turning bright red.

The Arch Magistrate laughed playfully. "My, she is refreshing isn't she?"

"Err, thank you," said Rosemary.

"People around here are often rather formal. I appreciate your candour. But to answer your question, the reason why we didn't just pop around for a cup of tea is that this situation is highly political. We can't have rumours of a treaty or a peace accord getting out in case it's sabotaged."

"Who would want to sabotage that?" Rosemary asked.

"Who indeed," said the Arch Magistrate. "However, we live in interesting times. And there are those among us in the magical world who would rather not have peace."

She looked around the room and Rosemary wondered whether she was thinking about the various magical parliamentarians gathered there. Was there a traitor in their midst?

"At any rate, we felt it best to keep the possibilities quiet, holding our cards close to our chest as it were, at least until we've reached the stage where key parties are ready to sign. I will speak to some of you individually." She looked at Dain and then at Burk.

Rosemary shuffled, distinctly uncomfortable. What had they signed up for?

"Until then," the Arch Magistrate continued, "you're free to enjoy the resort. But do come to the gala tonight, as there are many here who would like to meet you. You may leave now and we'll begin our parliamentary session."

They wandered out of the Great Hall and Rosemary was still feeling somewhat bewildered. "What do you think all that was all about?" she asked.

Athena sighed. "It sounded perfectly obvious to me."

"But what was it really about? Do you think it's as simple as she said?"

"You're implying it's some kind of trap?" said Dain. "I like a good trap."

Rosemary shot him an unimpressed look. "Settle down, pixie man."

"Hey, I take offense to that." Dain scowled and then flashed a cheeky smile. "Race you to the pool!"

He took off and Athena followed, leaving Rosemary walking next to Burk.

"And what did you think?" she asked.

"Well, the rumours I heard were true and more. This could be a game changer."

"Really?" Rosemary said as they walked. "I didn't think vampires were affected by witching politics."

"From time to time we are. Besides, it's not just witch politics, is it? Remember that message we received from the fae?"

"How could I forget?" said Rosemary. "Any idea who she was?"

"No record," said Burk. "It leaves me feeling uneasy."

"Athena got given a feather. Same kind. I have it up in my room in a plastic bag if you need it."

Athena had informed Rosemary of the visit from Finnigan and seemed oddly uncomfortable about it. Rosemary had chosen not to ask too many questions, but had taken the feather from the fae carefully to preserve evidence until she could show Burk.

"I'm not sure if it'll have any useful traces on it," said Burk. "But thanks for letting me know. I'll take a look at it later."

"I could show you now if you like," said Rosemary, taking hold of his hand suggestively.

Her tummy took that moment to make a loud growling noise.

"As tempting as that sounds, I think you need to eat first."

"Room service?" Rosemary suggested.

"How about we go to this gala and figure out what it's all about? And then maybe we can spend some alone time in my hotel room tonight."

"Sounds delightful." Rosemary smiled. "But why wait?"

Burk had a serious expression. "I'm afraid I'll need to report back on what we just heard."

"Of course. Never mind." Rosemary deflated.

"Rest assured you are a priority for me. And I'm very much looking forward to spending more time with you."

Rosemary smiled at him and said goodbye.

As she wandered back towards the main restaurant to get find some lunch, she noticed an old woman, dressed in a shabby cloak, with a distressed expression on her face as she tried to talk to the fancy witches as they walked past.

"Can I help you with something?" Rosemary asked, flashing the woman a warm smile.

The old woman's eyes lit up and she smiled, though it looked more like a grimace. She held out a weather-beaten leather bag. "I've lost my spectacles, deary. I'm sure they were somewhere in 'ere, only I can't find 'em...probably because I can't blimmin' see without 'em!"

"Is there anything I can do to help?" Rosemary felt sorry for the poor old creature. Clearly none of the hoity-toity Bermuda parliamentarians would stoop to help her.

"If you don't mind, just take a look in 'ere for me, will you?"

Rosemary bent down towards the bag. It was dark inside and seemed to be bigger than the outside suggested.

She reached in and fumbled around for a moment, before finding something about the size and shape of a glasses case.

She pulled it out, feeling somewhat dazed. "Is this it?"

"Oh my," said the old woman, grinning. "That sure is, deary. Thanks for your 'elp!"

The woman toddled away. Perhaps it was the low blood sugar, or maybe she'd stood up too fast, but Rosemary was feeling rather dizzy, though it was nothing a large hamburger wouldn't fix.

She decided to go have lunch and then for a quick dip in the pool with Athena. They spent time relaxing in the late afternoon sun.

Rosemary sipped a sunset coloured cocktail, letting her mind wander to fantasies of a certain handsome vampire.

She was struck again by how much she wanted him, and in a serious way. Would it be possible for them to have a real relationship? Even the word was terrifying to Rosemary.

Perhaps a fleeting casual thing would be safer. Either way, she was hooked.

Twenty

Rosemary and Athena arrived in their fancy dresses at the gala which was held in the grand dining room in the resort part of the complex not too far from the pool.

Rosemary wore the dress she'd chosen for Neve and Nesta's wedding, while Athena had opted for her ball gown, though it almost made her cry when she'd first put it on because of the memories of Elise and the fun and magical night they'd had at the druids' Summer Ball.

Rosemary had suggested she change, but Athena just shook her head sadly.

"All my clothes remind me of Elise, in a way," she said. "I'll cope." And indeed Athena did seem to be coping.

They met up with Dain and Burk at the entrance of the gala, which was adorned with orchids, surrounding the doorway to the resort's ballroom.

"Can't stay long," said Dain, looking rather more flustered than usual.

"What's going on? Trouble in paradise?" Rosemary asked.

"That head witch's number one bureaucrat tracked me down earlier," said Dain, "and requested I go on a secret mission."

"It's not to the fae realm, is it?" Athena asked.

"It's secret," said Dain. "But yeah, I guess. Pretty obvious, isn't it?"

"Dangerous, more like," said Rosemary. "You were kidnapped and locked up there for months."

Dain shrugged. "I think it was more like a month and a half, at least in your time."

"Either way, Dad," said Athena. "It's still rather dangerous when the countess is after you. Besides, she could be the one sending these feathery messages."

"Leithrein? She could be," said Dain, scratching his chin. "But I can't think why. She's only ever really been interested in the politics of their realm. Nothing over here."

"Maybe she's trying to get revenge," Rosemary muttered. "You know, after that cream incident where we tricked her into sending us back."

Dain laughed. "That was a riot. Anyway, I'm up for the adventure and I'll be careful. I'll do a little mingling at the gala, and then I'll be off." He tugged at his bow tie.

Rosemary realized he was dressed rather more sharply than usual. "What is it exactly that you're going to do?"

"Diplomatic mission," said Dain.

"Sounds fancy." Athena smiled.

"Yeah, well, I can't tell you I'm looking forward to it, but the magistrate was pretty convincing."

"What's your hesitation if it's not danger?" Rosemary asked.

Dain grimaced. "I haven't seen the family in years. Not since I was a child, really. Can't imagine they'll be pleased or welcome me home, no questions asked."

"The family." Athena narrowed her eyes. "Why have you never told me about them?"

"You know as well as I do it's hard to speak of the fae realm because of the magic. Even this conversation alone has caused me a few twinges of pain."

"I forget," said Rosemary. "But I suppose that's fae magic too. Oh well. Best of luck."

Dain tipped his bowler hat her and Athena. "Time to mingle." He strode off.

"He's a strange one," Rosemary muttered.

Athena smirked. "You're telling me."

Burk raised his elbow for Rosemary to take. "Shall we?"

As they entered the gala, Rosemary was relieved to not be wandering in alone, especially as the crowd was in rather fancy attire.

"Here's trouble," said Athena quietly.

"What?" Rosemary looked around just in time to see Elamina turn her head towards them with a stricken expression. She and Derse were standing next to two very uptight looking older people, dressed in excessively elaborate attire.

"The family," said Rosemary flatly.

"I'll leave you to it. I don't want to make your family reunion any more awkward," Burk said. He gave Rosemary's arm a quick squeeze and disappeared.

"Oh," Elamina said, stepping towards them. "Mamma, Pappa, of course you know Rosemary, and may I introduce you to Athena, my young cousin, and I suppose your great niece."

Elamina's parents, Ada and Warkworth, stared for a moment.

Rosemary coughed. "Err. Nice to see you Auntie Ada, Uncle Warkworth."

"Is it?" said Ada, giving them a frosty look.

Rosemary laughed. "Well, at least your pretences don't spread as far as being polite."

Athena looked at her mischievously. *I thought you said their names were Celil and Cecilia,* her voice sounded in Rosemary's mind.

That was granny's pet name for them. I think is was some kind of inside joke.

Athena covered her mouth so as not to laugh. *Granny does have a sense of humour!*

"Oh, come now," said Warkworth, stroking his silvering moustache. "We're just surprised."

"Surprised?" Athena asked. "Weren't you there today in the parliament? Couldn't you see us?"

"We were surprised then, too," said Ada coldly.

"So this is the one who's some kind of priestess, is it?" said Warkworth, eyeing Athena up.

"Some kind of fae princess," Ada corrected.

"I see." He began rubbing his chin more seriously. "Yes, I see how that could be to our business advantage."

"Excuse me," said Rosemary, feeling like she and her daughter were animals in a zoo.

"And you," said Ada. "You inherited *my* mother's magic."

"That's right." Rosemary beamed. "I've almost got the hang of it, too."

"Such a pity," said Ada.

Rosemary was almost done stifling her rage and was about to let loose on her hoity-toity family when Athena began talking in a rather too friendly way.

"So what do you think of this treaty?" Athena asked. "In favour or against?"

It sounded like she was making small talk, but Rosemary sensed a hidden motive and decided to play along. Athena was trying to gather more information to unravel the mystery of who could be thwarting attempts at peace.

It all started to make sense in her mind: the cancelled trip to Bermuda, the purple feathers planted for them to find...somebody was behind all of it.

"Nasty business," Ada muttered.

"It will be good for trade," said Warkworth, with a grin. "And if it's good for trade, then it'll be good for us."

He gripped the front pocket of his black and silver brocade waistcoat and chortled as if he'd made some kind of great joke.

"Yes, yes," Ada said. She nodded and waved them away, as if they were some kind of servants.

Rosemary and Athena walked off, looking at each other with confused expressions.

"So that's where Elamina gets it from," said Athena.

"I'm afraid so." Rosemary smiled apologetically. "They're terribly self-involved, aren't they?"

"So snobby and cold," said Athena. "Especially Ada. I can't believe she's Granny's daughter...It's like they're so wrapped up in their own power and money they don't even consider us people."

"That's my impression, too," said Rosemary. "I haven't seen them in a long, long time, but I don't remember them being any better when I was a child."

"I feel almost sorry for their kids," said Athena. "Imagine having parents like that. What kind of life would that be? So obsessed with prestige that you don't have anything else of value in your life. Nothing warm or meaningful."

"You're sounding very wise, love." Rosemary smiled at her daughter.

Athena smirked. "That's what they mean when they say 'blue blooded' isn't it? I can kind of understand that expression now."

"Aren't you glad you have me for a mother instead of parents like that?"

"Absolutely," said Athena. "Oh look, somebody else is approaching us."

"You there," said a haughty voice.

Rosemary turned to see an older woman with deep mahogany hair piled high up on her head in an elaborate hair-style. She was wearing a black and silver ballgown that looked almost Victorian in style. "You are the Thorn girls, aren't you?"

"Yes," said Rosemary.

"Ernest!" the woman called. "Come over here."

A man in a top hat joined her. "What is it, Cecily?"

"Here are the troublemakers," the woman explained.

"Excuse me?" Rosemary raised her eyebrows. "You're calling us troublemakers?"

The man laughed awkwardly. "Excuse my wife," he said with a slithery smile that made Rosemary uncomfortable. "She doesn't have much of a filter. I'm afraid that I think our little Beryl has told us something about you."

Athena gasped. "You're Beryl's parents? Oh, well that makes sense." She visibly bit her lower lip as if trying to hold back from saying anymore. *I suppose now we know where Granny got that pet name from! I bet it was a play on Cecily.*

Rosemary smiled awkwardly. *I bet you're right.*

"I hear you're instrumental to the treaty," Cecily said icily.

"Now, now. Don't start with that," said Ernest.

"Start with what?" Rosemary asked.

"Well, if you must know, it's a terrible idea," said Cecily. "Imagine the witches – clearly the ruling class of magical beings – deigning to lower ourselves to a vote with fae, druids...even *vampires.*"

She looked disgusted.

Rosemary tried not to laugh. "Does that concern you?"

"It's not the way things are done," said Ernest, frowning. "We must maintain our supremacy."

Rosemary and Athena looked at each other, mortified.

"Surely you must understand," said Cecily. "Don't get involved in any of that hullabaloo. I know you and Beryl have had your differences, but it's important for a united front. Perhaps we can even join forces..."

"I think I'm all right, thanks," said Athena.

"No, not really my cup of tea...the supremacy," said Rosemary. "Speaking of tea, I think we need some refreshments."

She grabbed Athena's arm and pulled her away.

"Oh my gosh!" Athena said as soon as they were out of earshot. "They're even worse than our family of elitist snobs. Now I feel sorry for Beryl too. I never thought that would happen in a million years."

"Indeed," said Rosemary. "I suspect the problem with this lot is they never talk to any *real* people. You know, they're all just socialising among themselves, not bothered to have a bit more of a diverse social life. If they did, they'd realize how ridiculous they all are."

"You're probably right," said Athena. "Do you think they might want to sabotage the treaty?"

"What do you mean – you're suspicious of them planting feathers and killing vampires and cancelling our flights?" Rosemary asked.

"I don't know," said Athena. "Maybe they'd be keen on partnering with somebody who would do that kind of nefarious thing."

"I guess it's a possibility," said Rosemary. "It's also possible that they're just boring people who think they're better than everyone else, while they're really just confined to their miserable, little snooty lives."

Athena laughed.

"What?"

Athena smiled at her mother. "I'm just so glad that we're not like that, that's all. Look, Dad's going." She pointed to the entranceway where Dain was waving to them and tipping his bowler hat again.

"I wish him luck," said Rosemary as Dain disappeared out through the doorway.

The music picked up and Burk reappeared, taking Rosemary by the elbow. "Care to dance?"

"Of course, I will," said Rosemary. After Athena had smiled and nodded and waved them away, they wandered onto the dance floor. The only couple there, not caring that the snobby witching folk in the room were staring at them.

"Not feeling too self-conscious?" Burk asked.

"Why should I care what any of them thinks?"

"It must be quite a sight. A witch and a vampire dancing in Bermuda. It's too bad Dain's not here. We could make it a threesome."

Rosemary gasped.

"I didn't mean that in the modern way," said Burk with a laugh.

"I'm very glad that you're not suggesting *that*," said Rosemary.

Burk tucked his hand slightly lower on her waist and pulled her closer, making Rosemary melt inside at the intimacy. "No, I'd much rather keep you all to myself. I have plans for this evening, you see..."

Rosemary smiled. "Care to share them?" she whispered in his ear.

"You'll just have to wait and find out." He held up her hand and twirled her around and then clutched her close again.

Time seemed to stop. That was how happy Rosemary felt in that moment.

And then a loud blast rent the air.

"Get down!" somebody shouted.

There were shrieks and crashing sounds. Everyone dived to the ground, covering their heads.

Rosemary's heart was in her throat, her pulse beating wildly as she looked around for Athena. Through all the chaos and fine silks, she caught sight of a familiar gold dress and crawled towards her daughter, at the edge of the dance floor, relieved to find her safe and sound.

"What was that?" Athena asked.

"Some kind of explosion," said Rosemary.

The building shook again.

Burk was next to them. "I'll get you outside," he said, and then Rosemary barely felt anything as the wind whisked past her and Athena. She marvelled at his strength to carry them both so quickly.

Burk placed them down on the edge of the beach, at a safe distance from the collapsing building as the chaos continued to ensue. More and more of the crowd were running outside. There were screams and yelling.

Another explosion sounded and the building collapsed further. Safety marshals with gold clipboards, dressed in fluorescent purple vests, ushered the confused parliamentarians to the assembly point not far from where Rosemary, Burk, and Athena stood. They seemed rather relaxed about the whole situation and assured the crowd everyone was safe and accounted for.

The purple in their vests reminded Rosemary of something

else that had been on her mind. She turned to Burk. "You don't think the countess could be behind all this? You know, she's been leaving those feathers around like calling cards. Could she have exploded the building?"

Burk shook his head. "I've been around a long time, but I've never seen fae magic like this. It seems like witches are responsible."

"So I guess we still have no idea what's going on then," said Athena.

Rosemary sighed. "Just when I was starting to enjoy myself. I should have known something like this was going to happen!"

Athena patted her shoulder. "I'm sure it'll all be fine."

"Fine doesn't seem to be the best way of describing this situation," said Rosemary as they continued to watch the chaos unfold.

"No, fine is not the right word, but I had to say something."

Rosemary shivered, despite the warm tropical evening. "I'm sure this must have something to do with the feathers, and maybe even those suspicious people they found on the beach after the Solstice."

Athena rolled her eyes. "But let me guess, whatever it is, we're going to get to the bottom of it?"

"Exactly."

Twenty-One

It was a hot day in Myrtlewood. Rosemary and Athena lay on the couches in the living room at Thorn Manor, feeling rather dejected.

They'd been evacuated from Bermuda the previous day and were recovering from jetlag, or whatever the magical equivalent of it was, while sipping iced tea.

"Sorry the holiday was short," said Rosemary. "We'll have to go somewhere else for a real holiday."

"Sounds like a good plan," said Athena. "I think we're going to need it."

Rosemary sighed. "You're right. Maybe the magical equivalent of world peace was too much of a stretch. Maybe I just want...to be empowered in my own life or something. I kind of do wish that they didn't evacuate us before we figured out what was going on. We've got no clues at all and it's not like her-royal-magistrate-librarian is going to tell us anything."

"What's with all the secrecy?" Athena asked. "I don't get it."

Rosemary rolled her eyes. "It seems a bit ridiculous, doesn't it? I mean, the whole parliament knows everything. I wonder if that was them."

"Who?"

"Oh, you know, your school frenemy's supremacist parents. Could it have been some kind of statement? Like a fundamentalist extremist wanting to blow things up."

Athena gave her a quizzical look. "I suppose it could be something like that. I mean, they'd have to feel pretty strongly about it if they were going to risk blowing up the witching Parliament resort, the height of their own snobby power, with them inside it!"

"Yes, that's true. Although they might have ducked out. And it was while the Arch Magistrate was entertaining witches, vampires, and whoever else was there. Maybe that's why they wanted to send a message."

"You think this was about us?" Athena asked.

"Maybe not on a personal level," said Rosemary. "I'm sure it's political though, and something to do with the treaty or the fact that there were other kinds of magical beings invited to Bermuda, like you and Dain and especially Burk. I don't think it was really about *me*. Although it's not like anyone there particularly likes me as a person." She crossed her arms and frowned.

"It's awful that somebody could attack us...attack me – just because of how I was born."

"So awful," said Rosemary. "But it does happen, possibly even in the witching world."

"It could be one of the other factions though. You know, like the fae or even the vampires or the druids."

"Druids are peaceful," Rosemary reminded her. "Except when they're misguidedly trying to abduct us for our own safety. Plus, Marjie told me the druids and witches have some kind of long standing peace accord – a mutual agreement not to get in each other's way. Druids are probably not even needed for this treaty."

"Maybe you're right. I didn't see any obvious druids there."

"Who knows the workings of global magical politics?" said Rosemary. "They're all beyond me. I'd rather keep it that way, to be quite frank."

They were interrupted by a knock on the lounge door.

"Excuse me," Gerald said, popping his head into the room. "I hope you don't mind. We've invited the Bible study group around."

"Okay," said Rosemary.

"Don't get up," said Mariana. "We know you're tired after your travels."

"People won't be here for another hour, at least," said Gerald.

"Oh, thanks for being so considerate," said Rosemary flatly. She didn't particularly want a random smattering of religious people at her house, especially not given the situation they'd just dealt with. Although she had to remind herself that her parents were the do-gooder types, not the fundamentalist explosion types. As far as she knew anyway.

She waved her parents away.

Athena groaned. "I suppose I should be going up to bed

anyway. Maybe I can do some painting first, just in case I need an outlet for my fae energy."

"How's it all going with the swooning?" Rosemary asked. "You seemed pretty normal in Bermuda."

"Actually, so far so good," said Athena. "In the entire day that we were away, nothing in particular happened."

"A long day wasn't it? It must be bedtime." She yawned.

"Are you still suspicious of Beryl's family?" Athena asked. "Do you think we should tell someone?"

"Who? The Arch Magistrate?"

"Yeah, or that top hat man."

"I don't trust him," said Rosemary. "He's in league with Elamina. And for all we know, our dear Bracewell-Thorn relatives might be just as culpable."

"Don't go getting paranoid about your cousin," said Athena. "You know that doesn't end well."

"Oh fine," said Rosemary. "But she's still a suspect as far as I can see. Maybe it's her awful parents."

"I wouldn't be too surprised if it was them," said Athena. "They seemed so cold and calculating, though they did say the treaty would be good for trade."

"It could be a ruse to put us off the scent."

Athena shrugged. "If you think they're clever enough to do that. I suspect they're too self-absorbed to think of anything like bothering to cover their tracks in front of us when they don't even treat us like human beings."

"Maybe you have a point," said Rosemary. "The time zones are messing with me. I'm afraid I need to have a nap." She pulled herself up and looked up the window. "Oh gosh, it's getting dark outside."

The doorbell rang and Rosemary groaned.

"Are you going to answer it?" Athena asked.

"It's probably just the Bible studies class arriving early."

They heard murmuring and laughter from the door and then Mariana said loudly, "Of course, she's right through here."

Rosemary and Athena looked at each other and then their mouths dropped as Burk walked into the room, flanked by Gerald and Mariana, who were both beaming at her.

"Rosemary, you have a gentleman caller!" said Gerald. "We won't leave you unchaperoned, don't worry." He nudged Burk, who gave him an odd look.

"Your parents?"

Rosemary shrugged apologetically.

"We'll just be in the kitchen if you need us, dear," said Mariana with a wink.

"Not really what I had in mind for our next date," said Burk with a laugh.

"What do you mean?" said Rosemary ironically. "You're just in time for Bible study class."

"Bible what?" said Burk.

"I'm sorry, did I fail to mention that my parents are extremely religious?"

"You might have said something in passing," said Burk.

Athena burst into laughter.

"They say meeting the parents is always awkward," Burk added with a shrug. "That wasn't too bad."

"Just you wait," Rosemary said. "They'll be grilling you in no time."

"I can't stay long enough for that, I'm afraid," said Burk.

"What are you here for?" Rosemary asked. "Is it important?"

Burk looked at Athena and then back to Rosemary.

"I'll just go upstairs," Athena said and scurried out of the room.

Rosemary gulped. "Not bad news, I hope?"

"I wanted to ask you on another date," said Burk.

"Oh, is that all?" said Rosemary with a sigh of relief. "I thought something terrible had happened again."

"Not quite the response I was looking for." Burk grinned.

"Oh, I mean, yes, of course. I would love that," Rosemary said. "What do you have in mind?"

"It's up to you," said Burk. "Would you like dinner at a fancy restaurant or another outing in nature?"

Rosemary narrowed her eyes at him. "You know, I've never been to your house."

"My...house?" said Burk.

"Yes. You've been here loads of times. You've never even mentioned where you live. Doesn't that strike you as odd?"

"My house is somewhat odd, actually," said Burk.

"Why is that?" Rosemary asked.

"Well, I live with my parents, you see."

"A grown man of over a thousand years old living with his parents?" Rosemary chortled. "I don't really mean to make fun of you but...actually...maybe I do mean to make fun of you," she said light-heartedly.

"Vampires tend to live in nests."

"Nests," said Rosemary. "That sounds kind of sordid."

"I assure you it is far from sordid. We just keep together so that we can take care of each other – a kind of stronghold, if you will – protecting ourselves from attack, protecting our assets."

"Okay," said Rosemary. "I get it. Some sort of vampire security club."

"If you like."

"So, can I go then?"

"You want to come to the Burk residence?"

"That's what you call it?"

"Sometimes," said Burk, sounding distinctively uncomfortable.

Rosemary laughed. "Yeah, maybe I do. You've met my parents, after all."

Burk looked anxious.

"Don't worry," said Rosemary. "I don't mean it as a kind of commitment thing or anything. We can keep things casual or whatever. It's not a marriage proposal or anything. I just want to see where you live."

Burk looked slightly deflated. "As you wish," he said. "How about tomorrow evening?"

"Sounds good," said Rosemary. "I look forward to it, and..."

Burk smiled. "You want to pick up where we left off in Bermuda?"

Rosemary grinned at him. "Perhaps. Would that be weird at your parents' house?"

"I assure you, it will not. I have my own wing of the castle."

"Ahh, a castle, of course," said Rosemary. "That does sound romantic."

"But if you prefer we could go somewhere else."

"The castle is fine," said Rosemary. "I don't have high standards or anything." She laughed.

Burk smiled back at her. "Until tomorrow, Rosemary," he said and left in a flash before her parents could interrogate him.

Twenty-Two

"You weren't exaggerating when you said castle," Rosemary muttered as Burk pulled down a long and windy driveway towards a large, dark, Gothic structure in the distance, complete with jagged towers. He had picked her up just after sunset and driven for about fifteen minutes through the countryside before reaching their destination.

"Why would I exaggerate about a thing like that?"

"I don't know. Don't all the guys brag about the size of their castles?"

"Perhaps this is a modern reference that I'm not quite familiar with," said Burk with a grin and chuckle that said he knew exactly what she was joking about. "So how were your parents after I left?"

"Gosh," said Rosemary. "They did grill me all about you. They wanted to know what you do for a living and were a little bit disappointed that you were a lawyer and not a church minister."

Burk laughed.

"And of course they want to know when the wedding bells are going to be ringing." Rosemary cackled. "As if that's ever going to happen."

Burk looked at her with a serious expression.

"What? You weren't about to propose to me right now on our fourth-and-a-half date, were you?"

"Of course not," said Burk.

"That's just as well, then," said Rosemary. "I'm not prepared for that level of commitment or co-dependency."

Burk coughed and changed the subject. "How's the shop doing?"

"Great," said Rosemary. "In fact, it's possibly better off without me. I arrived there today and Papa Jack shooed me away saying I hadn't had enough rest yet and that he has everything under control."

"Wow. That sounds promising."

"It's wonderful. Isn't it?" said Rosemary. "That means maybe we could go away on a proper holiday. Just me and Athena. Will you miss me?"

"Of course I will."

Rosemary batted her eyelids and laughed. "You don't seem to miss me much when you're away for work."

"Rosemary, I think of you frequently. Just because my instinct isn't to use modern technology to keep in touch every instant, don't think for a second that I don't miss you. I even think of writing you letters."

Rosemary looked at him. "You seem uncharacteristically sentimental today."

Burk shrugged. "Letters are how people stayed in touch for thousands of years."

"So why don't you write?"

"I assumed you'd find it unusual." He gestured out the window. "Here we are."

"I like unusual."

He left the vehicle and in a flash he was opening Rosemary's door, taking her hand, and leading her out of the car towards the entrance to the castle.

"I must confess, when you said nest I thought it was going to be some kind of underground hovel," Rosemary admitted. "Nothing so grand."

"We've been around a long time," said Burk.

"With plenty of opportunities to amass resources, I guess," Rosemary said nervously. "What kind of arsenal do you have in there?"

"You might not like the answer to that question," said Burk.

"Okay, then!" said Rosemary. "Time to change the subject again."

They walked up the steps towards enormous grey-and-black doors which began to open. A woman with long flowing black wavy hair and an hourglass figure stood there in a shimmery black dress. "Welcome," she said.

"Mamma," said Burk. "Don't trouble yourself."

"What?" said the woman, batting her overly long eyelashes.

"Rosemary..."

"This is your mother?" Rosemary asked.

"In a manner of speaking," said Burk.

The woman looked at least a couple of years younger than Rosemary. She gulped. She stared at the woman's mesmerising eyes.

"I wanted to meet your date," Burk's mother said. "It's been decades since you brought anyone to the house, centuries even..." She folded her arms. "Aren't you going to introduce me?"

"Rosemary, this is my mother, Azalea."

Rosemary smiled. "Nice to meet you."

"Nice?" Azalea said, as if she had a bitter taste in her mouth. "I don't like that word...*Nice*. Can't we say something more glamorous?"

Rosemary stiffened, sensing danger.

"It's an honour to make your acquaintance, perhaps?" Azalea suggested. "Or how perfectly frightful to meet you." She smiled with a wicked gleam in her eye.

Rosemary nodded. "Yes, either of those will do."

"Splendid," said Azalea, clapping her hands together. She glanced at Burk. "I like her."

Burk smiled. "So do I, Mamma. So don't go scaring her away."

Azalea laughed as if he'd just made a particularly clever joke. Then she turned away. "I'll leave you to your privacy," she said and then disappeared into a puff of black smoke.

"Wow. Can *you* do that?" Rosemary asked as Burk ushered her inside. She looked up at the high ceilings, and then around at the décor, which seemed positively medieval, tapestries included.

"It's one of Mamma's parlour tricks. She's got a rather odd sense of humour. She styles herself on the Addams Family."

"You don't say." Rosemary laughed.

"Or perhaps they're styled on her. We lived in New York in the early-mid twentieth century and she swears Charles Addams fell wildly in love with her at a socialite dinner party and wrote her fan letters for years after, though I've never seen any evidence."

Rosemary's jaw dropped. "You're saying Morticia Addams is based on your mother?"

"I can neither confirm nor deny."

"That was the exact vibe I was getting. I must say I'm a fan."

"That's just as well," said Burk. "However, my mother has scared off a number of friends before."

"Friends or dates?" Rosemary asked.

"Both, actually. None have visited the house for quite some time, as she mentioned."

"Is that why you never invited me over before?" Rosemary asked. "Were you worried your goth princess of a mother would scare me off?"

"I should have known better than to worry about a silly thing like that with you. You've got enough attitude to take on the whole clan at the same time."

"What does that mean?" Rosemary raised her eyebrows, unsure if she should be offended.

"It's a good thing. Believe me."

He led her along a dark, high-ceilinged stone passageway, lined with old oil paintings, most of them moody landscapes or haunting portraits of people in historic dress. "This is the way to the northern wing."

"Your wing?" Rosemary asked.

"Yes," said Burk, leading her along several more passages that became progressively more light and modern, until they reached a winding stone staircase.

She followed him up into a tower room with a panoramic view. In the centre, a simple round table with seating was laid out with a single silver dome on one side.

He pulled out the chair on that side of the table for Rosemary to sit, and then removed the dome to reveal a beautifully cooked succulent half chicken along with vegetables and various other additions.

"It looks good," said Rosemary. "I don't think I can eat half a bird."

Burk shrugged. "I'm a little uncertain on portions. It's been a long time since I've eaten food as a human."

"Do you miss it?" Rosemary asked as he uncorked an expensive looking bottle of wine and began to pour it into glasses.

"Only a little. I still get to enjoy most of my senses."

"Hey," said Rosemary, taking a sip of red wine, "you drink red wine but not champagne?"

"I suppose it's a bit like blood."

Rosemary grimaced. "I can't say we have quite the same tastes."

"That helps to keep things interesting. Now...tell me more. What's going on for you?"

Rosemary filled him in on her various paranoid suspicions regarding Bermuda and the treaty and the various snobby witches and the possibility of supremacist magical bombers.

He smiled and took it all in.

"What's on your mind?" she asked.

"You." Burk put down his glass and looked her in the eye, making Rosemary's insides quiver in a way that had nothing to do with imagining the taste of blood. "And this pleasant evening we're having," he continued.

"It is rather lovely, isn't it?"

A warm feeling spread across her, which was only partly to do with the wine.

"It's nice to get to know you better," she said. "And it was even nice to meet your mother, though I better come up with more words she doesn't detest as descriptive terms. She's so interesting. Did she...*make* you?"

Burk coughed. "Not exactly the conversation I had in mind. But, no she didn't."

"Then how is she your..."

"Azealia is mated to my sire."

"Mated...right. And your sire, you mentioned this before, didn't you?" Rosemary said. "Basically your vampy father."

"In a manner of speaking."

"I don't mean to ruin the mood with all this talk of your family, but I can't help it. I'm curious. Am I going to meet him too?"

"Perhaps one day," said Burk with a hopeful note in his voice. "He keeps to himself most of the time. He's often busy with matters of the vampire council."

"So that's why they chose you as an emissary?" Rosemary said. "Because of your father?"

"I believe so," said Burk. "But this is not quite the conversation I had in mind for this evening."

"You didn't bring me here just to talk about your parents?"

Rosemary asked. "How surprising. So what did you happen to have in mind, Mr. Perseus Burk?" She took another bite of the succulent chicken breast and a swig of wine.

"I'm trying to hold myself back," he replied.

Rosemary almost choked on her food. She put the cutlery down.

"No, keep eating," said Burk. "I want to make sure you have energy for the evening ahead."

Rosemary laughed. "I'm afraid I've rather lost my appetite... for food at least."

She felt a tingling deep inside.

She stood up and reached for Burk. A moment later they were locked in an intimate embrace with kisses that made Rosemary's world melt away and sensations that blew her mind.

She lost track of time entirely as her senses took over. And her body was well and truly satisfied in ways that had nothing in particular to do with the meal.

Hours later she found herself thoroughly sated, lying against the white silk sheets of Burk's ornate four poster bed.

He lay with her, gazing at her.

"What is it?" she asked, shifting her gaze from the view of the hills and forests outside to the handsome vampire looking at her.

"You're beautiful," he said.

Rosemary blushed. "Err. Thank you...and thanks for this, as well."

"For what?"

"For tonight. It was everything I could have hoped and more. Oh my gosh, my body's going to be aching for weeks."

Burk looked away, ashen faced. "I don't want you to think of it that way."

He stared off out the window into the distance.

"What do you mean?" Rosemary asked.

"I don't want you to think of it as just something I've given you, like a transaction. I want to be with you, Rosemary...whatever that means. I want to have a relationship with you. I know you keep making jokes about commitment, but you need to know, this isn't casual for me."

Rosemary felt a tightening in her chest.

She thought she'd wanted that too, at least at times. She'd never been particularly interested in casual dating, it seemed like too much effort with little reward. And she knew she wanted Burk. But now, faced with the earnestness in Burk's voice and the expectation, she was terrified.

"Maybe we should talk about this another time," said Rosemary.

"As you wish."

Twenty-Three

Rosemary sipped a cup of tea as she sat at the kitchen table at Thorn Manor with Tamsyn.

"I still don't think this is going to work," Tamsyn said, ruffling her greying blonde hair.

"We might as well give it a shot," said Rosemary. "After all, you have the special family magic for finding things."

"Things maybe, but what you're trying to do is reveal an entire mystery. I've never done anything like this before. I don't even know if my parents would've known how to do it at their prime."

Rosemary and Tamsyn had spent the morning going over the possibilities. They'd even assembled a range of magical ingredients and worked out a way that might be able to help them figure out what was going on with the magical politics.

Tamsyn had already tried several times to find the person responsible for the explosions in Bermuda, to no avail. The spell had simply fizzled in mid-air, leaving them to reconsider their options.

"This is just like when I tried to find Papa Jack's son," said Tamsyn. "Instead of a clear answer I just got fog, and now this! My magic really isn't all that I hoped."

"Maybe it's a group," Rosemary suggested. "It could even be the same group who took Papa Jack's son."

Tamsyn shook her head. "That sounds like a stretch, but this politics situation...well, it could be a group responsible."

Rosemary frowned. "I would assume the Bloodstone Society were involved, only they're safely locked away. At least, the key players who are interested in restoring the society to its full power are."

"You don't think they might have done it as a clever trick?" Tamsyn asked.

"What do you mean?" said Rosemary.

"You know, pretended the explosion was some sort of statement when really they were sneaking people out of the dungeons?"

"The prisoners? I don't think so," said Rosemary. "I get the feeling we would have heard something if Geneviève had escaped. She's not exactly subtle."

"Well, my magic seems to be of no use."

"Oh, I'm sure that's not true. We just have to keep trying. Come on. Let's give the revealing spell a try. I'm sure with your help, I'll have a much greater chance of getting it to work. It won't take long since we're already set up."

They'd set up the bundles of thyme, valerian, and sage in the lounge and interspersed them with tiger's eye crystals and lode-stones, all laid out in order.

Tamsyn finished her tea. "Right then, let's do it now. I've got to go and pick up Elowen soon from Neve and Nesta's house."

Rosemary took the teacups to the sink and then led Tamsyn back into the lounge only to find all their carefully laid out herbs and crystals in disarray.

"Oh no," said Rosemary. "We've been sabotaged!"

"What's that?" Athena called out, running into the room.

"Somebody's been in here," said Rosemary. "It wasn't you, was it?"

Athena frowned. "Of course not. I wouldn't go messing with another witch's crystals and herbs. You should know that."

"Then we've had an invasion!" Rosemary gasped. "Maybe whoever was behind the explosion is still in Thorn Manor somewhere."

"What's this about an explosion?" Gerald asked, wandering into the room with a broom in his hand.

Mariana was close behind. She laughed. "Oh, sorry for the mess."

"It does look like a bomb's gone off in here, doesn't it?" said Gerald. "Sorry. We were a bit concerned, is all."

Rosemary's jaw dropped. "You didn't do this. Did you?"

"Well, as a matter of fact..." said Mariana.

"Don't overreact, dear," said Gerald. "We were worried that your grandmother might have gotten to you."

"She was always getting carried away with her charms and other satanic things," Mariana added.

"It's not satanic," said Rosemary. "It's just that I was trying... to do something."

She was at a loss for how to explain the situation.

"What were you trying to do, dear?" Gerald asked.

"We're all ears," said Mariana.

Rosemary felt rage boiling and her blood. "This is *my* house, and as guests here you have absolutely no rights to be interrupting anything that I'm doing, nor do I have to tell you what it is!"

Gerald and Mariana looked at each other and then back to Rosemary.

"We're sorry," said Mariana.

"We didn't realize it was so important," Gerald added. "We're just looking out for you."

"Out!" said Rosemary.

"What?" her parents both asked.

"But, darling," said Mariana. "We're just here to help."

"You absolutely are not helping," said Rosemary. "You're just meddling. And I don't want you here."

Gerald and Mariana both looked at the ground, crestfallen. Rosemary almost felt sorry for them. Only the anger in her blood still boiled over, distracting her from any possibility of pity.

"We *are* sorry," said Mariana.

"I didn't realize it was so important to you," Gerald added.

"It doesn't matter," said Rosemary. "You're leaving. I'm sick of your sanctimonious rubbish. Go and pack your bags right now. I don't want you in my house."

"All right," said Gerald sadly. "We know when we're not wanted."

"I'm sorry if we overstayed our welcome, dear," said Mariana. "We'll just be heading back to Stratton."

They turned and walked away.

"That was a bit harsh, Mum," said Athena. "You know they don't understand any of this."

"That's no excuse," said Rosemary. "What they did was crossing a boundary. And it's about time I learned to stand up to them, anyway."

Athena patted her on the back. "Yeah, good job."

They tried to rearrange the ingredients and perform the spell again several times, though it was no use and Tamsyn had to leave.

Rosemary sighed and collapsed on the couch. "Magic doesn't solve everything, I guess."

Athena brought her a fresh cup of tea.

"They've gone," she said.

"Who?" Rosemary asked.

"Your parents, of course."

"Good...I'm glad they listened for a change."

"I can't say I'm sorry to see them leave," said Athena. "But I do kind of feel bad about how it happened."

"I probably could have been kinder. Maybe I could have been braver, too. I should have been more upfront with them all along and then I wouldn't have had to have snapped like that."

"Oh well," said Athena. "Another life lesson."

Twenty-Four

Athena stood at the counter of Myrtlewood Chocolates, serving a young rosy-cheeked child who'd come in with his grandmother. She handed over the little purple bag and the child, who looked to be about four years old, beamed at her.

"Matching!" he said, pointing to the bag and to Athena in the lavender apron she wore, and then around the shop to the similarly toned décor.

"That's right," said Athena.

The child clapped his hands and then pulled his grand-mother out of the shop calling, "Park! Time to go to the park and play!"

Athena laughed. "I could get used to this," she muttered.

"You're a natural, you are," said Papa Jack, poking his head out of the kitchen. "We can tell Rosemary she's no longer needed. She can have a rest."

Athena smiled at him. "I don't mind helping out, but I'll be back at school in a week and a half."

"Oh well," said Papa Jack. "I suppose we can have Rosemary back after all. As long as she's having a good lie down while you're here."

"I suspect she's pacing around, fretting, actually," said Athena. "Knowing Mum. But you're right, she does need a good rest and I quite like it here."

"Fancy a hot chocolate?" Papa Jack asked.

"Actually, I'd quite like a cup of tea."

"I'll put the kettle on," said Papa Jack and ducked back into the kitchen.

Athena had volunteered to help out to give her mother a break and also to test herself. She needed to see whether her fae-coming-of-age-infatuation-chaos, as she'd started referring to it, was under control. This was especially important given that her seventeenth birthday party was quickly approaching and she did not want to miss out.

Though, despite all her worries, she did quite enjoy working in the chocolate shop as she'd told Papa Jack.

Just then, a familiar face appeared. Felix entered the shop with a moony look in his eyes.

Oh dear, Athena thought. *Maybe I jinxed it.*

"Not happy to see me?" Felix asked, clearly noting the look on Athena's face.

"Erm...uhh..."

Felix squinted and looked around. "Hey, are you playing dryad death metal? This band is really good."

Athena laughed, breaking the tension. "Blame Covvey's

magical music field for that one."

Felix looked momentarily baffled.

"Never mind," said Athena. "It's not that I don't want to see you in particular, it's just that—"

"Oh yes, I'm sorry. I heard about the situation with Elise," said Felix.

"You did?"

"Uhh, yes," said Felix.

"Oh," said Athena, looking down at the counter.

"That's why I wanted to see you," he continued. "I thought I might be able to cheer you up."

There was a twinkle in his eye that made Athena distinctly uncomfortable, along with the nonchalant way he was leaning against the side of the counter.

"Felix, are you flirting with me?" Athena asked.

"I might be giving it a whirl," he said.

She glared at him. "This is totally inappropriate. You know I'm going through a break-up with one of your best friends."

"Yes," said Felix, gazing dreamily at her. "But you and me... think about it. We shared a moment the other day at the ice cream parlour."

"Felix, I hate to tell you this, but it was just my fae magic playing up."

"I know," said Felix. "But—"

"What? Who told you?"

"Well, Elise did actually."

Athena felt a sting of betrayal at her privacy being compromised like that without her consent.

"Oh, I see," she said.

"Not like that," said Felix. "We badgered it out of her. Deron was getting righteously angry at whoever had made her cry so much, he wanted revenge, but then it turned out it was you...and it was out of your control."

"Right," said Athena. "Well, I suppose it's better people know so they can stop me making a fool of myself."

"Care to make a fool of yourself with me?" Felix said, batting his eyelashes as he leaned further onto the counter.

"Felix!" Athena said crossly. "I told you this is fae magic. You're under its spell. It's not real, and besides, what about Ash?"

"Ash?"

"Yes, you know, our friend Ashwagandha, who you went to the ball with."

"Oh, Athena...dear sweet Athena, you know nothing was ever going to happen there. Ash is too good for me."

"And as for me?"

"You're rotten to the core, just like me," said Felix cheekily.

Athena knew he was only ribbing her, but his words struck an uncomfortable chord. She did have a strong feeling there was something deeply wrong with her, just like her father who struggled to function in the human world, or maybe even worse. At least with Dain you knew what you were getting. Athena worried her wrongness was more dangerous because it was buried so deep.

*Maybe that's the real reason Elise left me...*she wondered. *She got too close, she could tell I wasn't good inside, or worse, she saw who I am and decided I just wasn't worth her time.*

"Felix, get out of here," said Athena, "before I get Papa Jack to chase you out with a spatula."

"But..."

"You're clearly bewitched."

"Athena, I had feelings for you before...a long time before all this fae enchantment stuff. It's real."

"I'm sorry, Felix," she said. "It's not real for me. You're a friend, and whatever it is you feel, it's not mutual."

As Felix wandered sadly out of the shop, his head hanging low, Athena had a pang of regret. Maybe her romantic life would be easier with someone as carefree and playful as Felix. *If only things were that simple.*

Then, a happy realisation struck her and she jumped for joy.

"Good news?" Papa Jack said, coming out of the kitchen with a tea tray.

"Something like that," said Athena. She was bubbling with satisfaction. All that time with Felix gazing at her and she hadn't once succumbed to the fae-infatuation-chaos.

I might just be getting the hang of this!

She picked up her tea cup and took a sip.

"You make an excellent Earl Grey," she said to Papa Jack.

He beamed at her, then turned towards the door as someone entered. "Oh deary me," he said.

Athena followed his gaze to see a man hobbling in. A very familiar man.

"Dad!" she called out, then came around from the counter to help him into a booth so he could sit.

Dain's hair was much more chaotic than usual and his clothing was torn.

"What happened?"

"The fae realm," Dain said.

Twenty-Five

Rosemary arrived at the chocolate shop quickly after receiving Athena's call to find that Dain had indeed returned from his trip to the fae realm looking much worse for wear.

"It was all much harder than I thought," Dain said, taking a sip of tea. He winced.

"Is that pain from injuries?" Athena asked. "Or is it from talking about the realm?"

"Hard to tell the difference," said Dain, sounding out of sorts.

"I suppose you can't tell us much, then," said Rosemary, feeling disappointed. She wanted to know if the fae were really behind the mysterious feathers and the death of that vampire girl, or whether they were being set up by someone else trying to throw them off the trail.

With Neve still away on her honeymoon with Nesta, the

local authorities weren't worth calling. Rosemary wasn't about to even attempt to explain her various wild speculations to Constable Perkins who would almost certainly suspect her instead.

"What can you tell us?" Athena asked.

"I, uhh," said Dain, clutching his ribs.

"Do we need to get you medical attention?" Rosemary asked, concerned.

"No, it's all superficial," Dain insisted. "I'll be fine in a few days. I wouldn't want to miss your sweet seventeenth." He smiled at his daughter.

"If it goes ahead," said Rosemary. "I'm worried it will just be a magnet for danger, and...well, the situation with Athena—"

"Mum, I'll be fine," Athena said, crossing her arms. "My little problem is under control, thank you very much. And I'm definitely having a party."

Rosemary sighed and turned her attention back to Dain. "You're looking better," she said in surprise. Indeed, he did seem to be recovering before their very eyes."

"I told you it was superficial," said Dain. "Anyway, what I can say is that I had a lot of trouble getting in."

"To the fae realm?" Athena asked.

Dain simply nodded, as if the words would be too hard to say. "I had help from powerful witches sent by the Arch Magistrate and everything, so combined with my fae magic it should have been simple, only..."

"What?" Athena asked.

"Their magic kept backfiring on them, and then the veil would shift around."

"Shift around?" Rosemary asked. "I thought it could be opened anywhere with the right magic."

"That's what I thought too," said Dain. "Only it kept disappearing on me."

"Someone was sabotaging your attempts," said Rosemary with certainty. "Maybe it was someone from Bermuda. I don't like that so many of those snobby witches are in Myrtlewood now that Bermuda has been evacuated."

"They are?" Dain asked. "I must have missed that part."

They filled Dain in on the explosions at the witching parliament resort.

"That's funny," said Dain. "I could have sworn she was behind all this."

"Who?" Rosemary and Athena asked simultaneously.

"Leithrien."

They looked at Dain blankly until he added, "You know. The Countess of West Eloria."

"Oh, the countess," said Rosemary. "I did sort of suspect her —what with the purple feathers and all."

"She doesn't want a treaty?" Athena asked.

"She's highly politically motivated," said Dain. "Which is why she kidnapped me. She wanted to have something to hold over my mother."

"Isn't your mother some sort of fae queen?" Rosemary asked. "Doesn't that make her more powerful than a dodgy little countess?"

Dain laughed. "My mother is *the* Fae Queen," he said. "And yes, she is powerful, my whole family are, which is probably why Leithrein never even let them know she had me."

"She was biding her time," Athena said sagely. "Waiting for a weakness in the fae monarchy so that she could use you as a weapon, and me too, I suppose, if she'd managed to detain me."

"You think she could be getting through the veil to sabotage the treaty?" Rosemary asked. "But how?"

"I did suspect that, at first," said Dain, taking another sip of the fresh cup of tea that Papa Jack had just brought him.

"But?" Athena asked as Rosemary took a long swig from her own teacup, wishing for something stronger.

"It can't be her," said Dain. "Fae can't produce explosions. They can barely create any kind of magical combustion in the fae realm, let alone here. Believe me, I've tried." He grinned.

"I bet you have," said Rosemary. "So you're sure it's not her?"

"She could be working with someone else," Athena suggested. "Maybe she's partnered with some powerful witches who don't want a treaty either."

Dain shook his head. "That's not her style at all. Leithrein doesn't have partners. She only has servants and she wouldn't stoop so low as to work with mere human witches, or any other magical species for that matter."

"Then it must be *them*," said Rosemary, giving Athena a meaningful look.

"Who?" Dain asked.

"Mum suspects these snobby witch supremacists," said Athena. "The parents of an awful girl at school."

"That Beryl you told me about?" Dain asked. "Could be...only."

"Only what?" Rosemary asked. "They have a clear motive."

"Sure," said Dain. "But don't fall into the trap of suspecting people of a crime just because you personally don't like them."

"So you're the expert now, are you?" Rosemary asked.

Dain grinned at her. "That's what always gets people in the crime dramas I've been watching."

Twenty-Six

Athena opened her eyes on the morning of her seventeenth birthday. The room was bright. Too bright. She'd closed the curtains the night before, but perhaps the house had opened them for her as it sometimes did.

She blinked and looked around. Something was different.

"Mum!" Athena called out.

"What is it love? Oh, and happy birthday!" Rosemary came into the room holding a tray of fancy breakfast foods.

Athena wanted to smile and thank her, but she had a bone to pick first.

"Have you been in my room, rearranging things while I was asleep?" she asked. "Something is different."

Rosemary shook her head, clearly baffled by the suggestion.

"No. I've been far too busy making you blueberry waffles with all the trimmings, so you could have a lovely birthday breakfast."

"Oh," Athena said. "But my bookshelf is gone...and there's a new one?"

She got out of bed to examine the new shelf. The small white one by her desk had vanished and taller mahogany shelves were now several steps away, full of her books.

"The house?" Rosemary suggested. "Maybe it made you a new bookshelf as a birthday present."

"That's sweet," said Athena, smiling. "And slightly odd. Wait a minute."

She took another step closer and the shelf began to move, swinging open like a door to reveal...

"A secret room!" Rosemary squealed.

"No way!"

Athena peeked into the new room that had merely been a blank space on her wall the day before. She was astonished to find it contained a library – half the books being her favourite kinds of fantasy and paranormal romance, only these were new titles she hadn't read yet – and the other half seemed to be magical non-fiction. There was a cosy purple velvet chair in the corner, and a little writing nook.

"Amazing!"

Rosemary sighed in delight. "It's like all my childhood dreams come true! Only, it's your room, not mine."

Athena grinned. "The house likes me best."

"Well, I'm not sure I can compete with the house," said Rosemary. "But here's your present."

Athena took the silver envelope from her mother and opened it up. "Plane tickets!"

"Yes," said Rosemary. "This is me making good on my

promise of a real holiday. They aren't real tickets – yet. But you get to choose the destination and we'll go on a proper holiday as soon as things in the shop are settled and we've resolved the latest bout of magical chaos."

"So you're thinking after Lughnasa but well before the Autumn Equinox?" Athena suggested.

"Exactly!"

Athena felt a tug of anxiety as she stepped out of the car on the night of her birthday. The day had gone smoothly enough. She'd slept in and then eaten a delicious breakfast in bed prepared by her mother and Marjie who had insisted on singing her "Happy Birthday," even though the attention made Athena blush.

Athena had felt slightly odd that morning, a kind of humming she attributed to the fae-infatuation-chaos peaking.

She'd spent the rest of the morning painting in an attempt to release as much pent up creative energy as possible. She'd been trying to capture the view of the forest and sea from her balcony for days, but her technique was still lacking. When she'd first started painting she'd improved rapidly, but she seemed to have hit a wall. It made her wonder whether she ought to enrol in proper classes.

Instead of finishing the landscape piece, she'd put it aside in favour of what she thought of as just messing around. She'd chosen a random assortment of colours and had deliberately zoned out, smudging the paint around, moving the brush without much thought. Occasionally images would appear which she attributed to her brain trying to make patterns where there were none. Eventually, she decided it was finished, just as her mother entered the room to check on her.

"Oh," said Rosemary. "That's different."

"It is a bit," said Athena. "But it seems to have been a good outlet. I feel almost normal now."

"Did you mean for her to look that disturbed?" Rosemary asked, staring at the painting.

"What?" said Athena, looking at the smudges of pink, purple, blue, and white. "What are you talking about?"

"The girl," said Rosemary, pointing to the side of the canvas.

Athena looked again. It took a moment, and a slight change of perspective, before she could see it. The painting did look to contain a disturbed looking face. A girl, screaming. "Well, that's a bit creepy," she said. "It must be just a coincidence."

Rosemary put her arm around Athena's shoulder. "Or a subconscious expression of teen angst."

"Whatever," Athena replied. "As long as it's nothing too magical. I need a break from all that."

Rosemary patted Athena on the back. "Tonight will just be a perfectly ordinary seventeenth birthday party," she assured her. "Despite that it's held in a magical town, in a magical pub..."

Later, Athena stood there, next to the car, in the beautiful emerald green silk dress Rosemary had given her as a present that morning after she'd handed Athena the fake plane tickets and the promise of a real holiday.

She looked across the road at the pub and wished for a fun evening with friends. Elise was still invited, and Athena hoped she'd be coming.

It could be my chance to patch things up with her, Athena thought, though she didn't want to get her hopes up.

"Are you okay, love?" Rosemary asked, coming to stand beside her.

"Just a little nervous," Athena admitted.

"I've got your back," said Rosemary. "I'll watch out for anything suspicious."

"Even if it's coming from me?" Athena asked.

"Especially from you," Rosemary reassured her.

Athena nodded and began walking towards the front entrance to the pub, but before she could reach it she noticed an odd bundle, off to the side of the steps. On closer inspection it was a person.

"Umm, hello?" she asked.

The person-bundle raised his head and Athena recognised Finnigan. She looked at her mother, who shook her head vigorously.

"We can't just leave him there," Athena hissed.

"Danger," Rosemary mouthed.

Ignoring her mother, Athena stepped closer.

"What are you doing here?" she asked Finnigan.

He was sprawled out on the ground. Athena noticed an empty bottle of cream off to one side. "Oh...no. You stupid boy."

"Athena?" he asked, bleary eyed. Then he hiccoughed. "They wouldn't let me in."

"Not in that state," said Rosemary. "You're wasted."

"Eugh," said Finnigan. "Not anymore. I'm coming down."

"I didn't know it affected you like that," Athena muttered.

Finnigan shrugged. "There's a lot you don't know about me, I guess. No one does."

He looked unbearably sad.

"Don't you have some place to go?" Rosemary asked.

"I have...nothing. No one," he said.

"You're pretty chummy with Beryl," said Athena.

"Beryl...was just using me to taunt you," said Finnigan. "You're clever enough to know that. Clever girl...you are...But Beryl...she let me stay at her big fancy house for a while, only her awful parents turned up with their snooty friends and turfed me out on the street."

He slumped over even more.

"Tell us about the feather," Rosemary said.

Athena shot her mother a look. Clearly this wasn't the right time to talk about feathers.

"What?" Rosemary whispered. "He might say more when he's under the influence."

"Feather...?" Finnigan asked.

"You gave me a feather, remember?" said Athena gently. "Tell us, was it from the countess or someone else?"

Finnigan laughed. "You got me," he said. "It wasn't a real message. I just wanted to see you. I found the feather in the woods near your house and thought it would be a good excuse..."

Athena's heart went out to him. He looked so hopeless, slumped there on the cobbled path with nowhere to go.

"What's going on here?" Dain said, coming to join them.

Athena gave him a brief run-down of the situation.

"So, young Finnigan," said Dain, taking a good look at the

boy. "You were the one who kidnapped me and led my daughter astray."

"Don't hurt him or anything," Rosemary said. "He's just a boy."

Dain crowed with laughter. Then he shook his head, still looking at the boy. "Nicely played, young chap. Come on. I'll help you up."

Dain hoisted Finnigan up to standing.

"Where will you take him?" Athena asked.

Dain paused for a moment. "I don't want to miss your party..." said Dain. "I know, I'll pop him in the corner with a lemonade for a few hours."

"And then what?" Rosemary asked, sounding appalled.

"Maybe he can stay at my place for a few days, give him a chance to sort himself out."

"But why?" Athena asked. "After everything he did. Why would you take him in like a stray puppy?"

"The poor young sap reminds me of myself," said Dain with a sad look in his eyes. "You two know more than most people how many times I fell off the rails and messed things up. Maybe... maybe this is a chance for me to redeem myself."

"That's kind of sweet," said Athena.

"Wait, you're actually suggesting you bring him into Athena's party?" Rosemary said, sounding cross.

"It's okay, Mum," said Athena. "I want him to. Better than leaving him out here on the ground."

Rosemary sighed. "I suppose so," she muttered. "But I don't like it.

They entered the pub to find it transformed.

"The decorations are beautiful," Athena said, grinning at Marjie.

Emerald green balloons hung from the ceiling, along with a flurry of elaborate green ribbons and silver paper stars that twinkled like real stars above them.

"It matches my dress!"

"Your mother might have let me in on the secret," said Marjie.

"We're almost finished setting up," said Sherry. "Happy birthday, love." She gave Athena a hug and handed her a little green velvet box.

"What's this?"

"Just a little something from me."

Athena opened the box to find teardrop shaped dangly earrings with emerald green glass.

"They're beautiful! Thank you."

"It's nothing," said Sherry. "I had them up in my room and just had the inspiration that they'd be the right thing to give you. They're not new, I'm afraid."

"It doesn't matter at all," said Athena. "It's even more personal this way."

Sherry beamed at her and Athena was relieved that she hugged Rosemary warmly too. Whatever residual shame Sherry seemed to hold about stealing the emerald pendant seemed to have vanished.

Athena clutched the pendant that she wore around her neck, hoping the magic would be enough to keep her from making a terrible fool of herself.

Friends started arriving. Pretty soon the pub had filled up with all of the friends from the town.

Ferg was wearing his characteristic Saturday brown tones with a backwards baseball cap and a knitted sweater, paired with matching shorts, knees socks, and sandals.

Sam, Ash, and Deron arrived with a rather sheepish looking Felix. Athena smiled at him and gave him a friendly hug.

"I'm glad we sorted all that out," Felix muttered.

"Me too," Athena said. "Behave yourself."

She looked around the room and then back to Sam. "No Elise?" she asked.

"I'm afraid not," said Sam.

Athena felt her shoulders sag.

"She might still be coming," Ash added. "She said she wasn't sure yet."

"I miss her so much," said Athena.

"I know," said Sam, giving her another hug.

Una and Ashwyn arrived with the foundling children, followed by Neve and Nesta just returned from the honeymoon in Spain and looking rather tanned and glowing. They had little Mei with them.

Tamsyn arrived shortly after with Elowen, meaning that all the foundling children were now in the room and seemed to be playing hide seek or something similar.

Even Mr. June, the mayor, made an appearance, despite Athena distinctly not inviting him at Rosemary's request.

"But the small town," said Athena. "You can't really control these things."

"I suppose not," said Rosemary. "I'd better go and talk to

Neve. I've got a lot to fill her in on." She dashed off towards the detective where she'd no doubt be talking about the various suspicions that always seemed to preoccupy her.

Athena noticed Liam was helping behind the bar while Sherry was handing around platters of nibbles.

Athena looked around and smiled. *It's amazing all these people here to celebrate me. Only a few months ago it was just me and Mum and now we've got a whole village.*

Rosemary smiled back at her from the other side of the room where she was talking to Neve. Then she turned at the sound of her name.

Elise was standing there behind her, dressed casually in a t-shirt and jeans.

Athena's eyes widened in surprise. "You came."

She reached forward to hug Elise, who stiffened and stepped back.

"Sorry," Athena said, standing back. "I just...I've missed you."

Elise smiled sadly. "I've missed you too. You look amazing."

"Uh, thanks."

"How's it all been going?"

"No major disasters," said Athena. "But it's not the easiest time in my life."

"I bet," said Elise. "And I'm sorry you have to deal with it alone."

"Not exactly alone," Athena said, gesturing around the room. "It looks like the whole town's here to support me."

She felt a bitterness that the one person she most wanted support from was keeping her at arm's length.

Elise smiled. "It's the beauty of Myrtlewood, isn't it? Sometimes it's a right pain to live in a small town, and then there's this nice sense of community about it."

Athena smiled slightly, feeling hopeful. She looked towards Elise. "I was thinking..."

Elise frowned. "Let's not talk right now. It's not the best time with all these people around and I'm still processing everything."

"Fair enough," said Athena, feeling slightly disappointed. She tried to rack her mind for the right words say, the ones that would bring Elise back, only all of her thoughts seemed to end in dead ends.

She caught sight of Finnigan over in the corner, slumped at a table. Dain was sitting next to him with two glasses of lemonade between them.

Athena smiled at her father and he grinned back. Things had come a long way with their relationship. Dain was still erratic but he was much easier to deal with now than before when he was hooked on cream.

She'd even grown to like his somewhat unusual responses to everything. It kept things interesting.

Sherry passed around a tray of her famous mulled mead. Athena took a sip of the delicious brew.

She was determined to enjoy the evening, despite the dark cloud hanging over them with magical politics and the like.

Suddenly the ambient music of the pub stopped and another sound broke through: the gentle strumming of a guitar.

Athena turned to the far corner of the room to see none other than the travelling minstrel.

"Oh, no," she said. "Not him."

Rosemary dashed over to her side.

"We booked him. Didn't we?" said Athena. "After everything that's happened…"

"I totally forgot," said Rosemary with a grimace. "I should have cancelled after the wedding incident."

Athena shrugged. "It's not like we had his contact details."

"I'll get rid of him," said Rosemary. She began wading towards him through the crowd.

It was too late. Everyone had begun dancing as the guitar music picked up and the minstrel started singing.

One moment Athena was experiencing dread and then the next she was swept up into a jig, feeling lively and free.

She danced with her friends, all around the room.

There was such joy.

"What a marvellous way to celebrate your birthday!" said Sam as they pressed their palm to Athena's and they walked around in some kind of folk dance that everyone somehow knew the steps to.

"It's glorious!" said Elise, clearly losing herself in the moment.

In the flurry of joyful dancing, Athena had never felt so free… except for a quiet ringing in the back of her mind which hinted at danger.

Twenty-Seven

Rosemary had been doing something just a moment ago, with determination. Quickly it felt like she was wading through treacle, then she was caught up in the thrill of dancing.

She saw Athena being swung around the room by Deron, and then everyone sort of fell in line into some kind of traditional medieval folk dance. It was all marvellous until Burk appeared at her side, tapping her on the shoulder.

"Rosemary, what's going on?"

"We're...dancing," said Rosemary, puzzled. "The dancing reminds me of something."

"You're all in a trance," said Burk. "That's what's going on. I thought I sensed it last time we were all here and that minstrel was playing. But this time, it's much worse. It's a bit like the sirens. You're all in thrall."

"Enthralled?" Rosemary muttered. She was standing still in

order to speak to Burk, but her feet were tapping a little jig beneath her. "I don't know what you're saying."

"Snap out of it," he said, reaching across towards a finished drink, the glass containing only ice. He plucked an ice cube out and held it to Rosemary's temple.

She felt a cold shock running through her as she realized Burk was right.

It wasn't the same kind of bewitching trance as the sirens had created, but it was something else. Some kind of frivolity connected to the music that was so easy to get swept up in.

"Athena," she said.

Her daughter was across the dance floor, crowded by others.

Rosemary waded through the people dancing till she reached her.

"Athena. We've been entranced. You've got to snap out of it. Snap out of it!"

"Mum," Athena said. "I'm having the time of my life. I just had five marriage proposals."

"Excuse me," said Rosemary.

Athena pointed around the room as if counting. "Yes, at least five suitors. Which one do I pick? Oh, maybe I could pick all five! Do you think they'd allow it?"

"No," said Rosemary. "Not at all. Go over to Burk. I'm going to find some ice."

"Oh, Mum. You're no fun," said Athena and danced off again.

"I've got to stop this," Rosemary said as she started wading towards the source of the chaos, the travelling minstrel. But the closer she moved, the thicker the air seemed to be, though she kept stepping, one foot in front the other.

She didn't feel she was making any progress at all. And the dancers kept getting in her way, knocking her back. Finally, the music stopped and Rosemary was able to move freely again.

She reached the edge of the room where the minstrel had been, only to find his seat vacated.

"Where has that little creep gone?" Rosemary muttered.

"Isn't he dreamy?" said Elise, standing next to her.

"Elise?" said Rosemary, reaching for another ice cube from a nearby glass and popping it to Elise's temple.

"Oh gosh, what was that?" Elise asked groggily, rubbing her eyes. "I feel all weird and tingly."

"It must be some kind of spell," said Rosemary. "We've got to find him."

"Where do you think he's gone?" She looked around the room, but the minstrel was nowhere in sight.

She caught Burk's gaze, and he pointed to the door.

Rosemary dashed towards it, but Burk was quicker. By the time she got outside he was standing in the pathway in front of Athena and the travelling minstrel, who were locked together, their fingers interlaced like lovers.

"Out of my way," said the minstrel.

"I'm afraid not," said Burk.

"Oh please let us go!" said Athena.

"Where do you think you're going?" Rosemary asked.

"To elope, of course, Mother," said Athena, twirling her hair around her finger with a wild gleam in her eyes.

"Excuse me?"

"Callum here is the love of my life."

"The name's Cailean, and yes. We are in love," said the minstrel.

"No you most certainly are not," said Rosemary.

"Of course we are," Athena argued. "It was love at first sight, wasn't it, baby?"

Rosemary felt nauseous as the two bewitched lovebirds gazed at each other dreamily and then kissed right there in front of them.

"Stop that, this instant!" Rosemary cried, trying to pull Athena away.

She pointed at Cailean. "Boy, have you got a lot to explain. What just happened in there with the music? That wasn't just ordinary fun. That was magic."

The minstrel smiled with a twinkle in his eye. "What can I say? It's a gift...And now my love and I will travel to share it with the world."

"You're both drunk on each other's magic," said Rosemary. "This will not do."

"What do you want me to do?" Burk asked as Cailean and Athena began kissing again.

"We've got to pull them apart!" said Rosemary.

"I cannot believe this," a voice said from behind her.

Rosemary turned to see Elise. "It's not her fault," Rosemary called after her as Elise ran off in tears. "Oh gosh, I knew this party was a bad idea."

She helped to pry her daughter away from Cailean, though Burk was so strong he didn't need the assistance.

"What do you want me to do with him?" said Burk, holding

the struggling minstrel using his thumb and index finger as though he was holding up a small piece of garbage. "The castle has a dungeon, you know."

Rosemary's eyes widened at that little titbit. "Just make sure he leaves town. If I ever see him again, it'll be too soon."

"As you wish," said Burk. "You're coming with me, buddy."

They were gone in a flash.

Rosemary led her daughter back into the pub. Athena still seemed as if she were in some kind of dream state and the ice didn't seem to help.

"It must be your fae magic," said Rosemary.

She tried another ice cube, unsuccessfully.

Una approached and waved a hand in front of Athena's dazed eyes. "Here, this might help." She pulled an ointment bottle from her bag and began to apply some pale purple cream to Athena's wrists and temples.

"Is that some kind of aromatherapy?" Rosemary asked.

"Something like that," said Una. "Bergamot oil lotion, it helps me when my fae magic gets a little bit out of control."

"This would have come in handy earlier," said Rosemary.

"Oh sorry. I totally forgot. I didn't return your text the other day. The kids have really been keeping us on our toes."

"It's okay," said Rosemary. "We managed to sort it out as much as we could, for now anyway."

Athena groaned. "Oh my gosh, what just happened?"

"You don't want to know," said Rosemary drily.

"Oh no. I didn't..."

"I'm afraid so."

"I'm never going to live this down," said Athena, burying her head against her forearm on the table in front of her.

"Don't worry," said Una. "Most people were so enchanted by the music that they won't have noticed anything odd."

"But Elise..." Athena turned to her mother.

Rosemary gritted her teeth. "I'm afraid she might have seen a little bit too much."

Athena groaned again. "My life is over."

"No, it certainly is not," said Rosemary. "It's just one day."

"It was supposed to be a good day," said Athena.

"Birthdays often aren't," said Una. "You know, it's your solar return, when the sun gets back to where it was when you were born."

"Of course," said Athena. "And to top it all off, now I smell like a teapot."

Rosemary laughed. "There are worse things."

Twenty-Eight

Athena refused to leave her room for days after her birthday. Rosemary didn't try to push her. It had been quite a shock to her system.

The party was a beautiful dream and a terrible nightmare all in one.

But aside from the awful embarrassment, it didn't seem too nefarious.

Rosemary spent days trying to figure out if there was a connection between the travelling minstrel and Athena's spell-binding magic and all of the global witching and fae politics that they seemed to be surrounded by, but could come up with no particular link between them.

"Just an unfortunate coincidence," Rosemary muttered to herself as she wiped down the counters in Myrtlewood Chocolates after a busy day.

"What's that?" Papa Jack asked.

"Oh, nothing," said Rosemary. "I'm just trying to figure out what's going on. It feels like there are all these puzzle pieces but they don't quite fit."

"Maybe they're different puzzles," said Papa Jack.

"That's the conclusion I've come to."

"You still look worried." Papa Jack put a hand on her shoulder. "But don't fret, my girl. Athena will be okay."

"You're so sure. Why is that?"

"I just have an instinct for these things," said Papa Jack sadly. "I had a terrible feeling the day my son went missing but..."

"What?"

"I didn't listen to my instincts. And I've never made that mistake since."

"It always pays to listen to your gut, doesn't it?" said Rosemary.

Papa Jack nodded sagely. "Now go home. Be with your girl. I'll finish up here."

Rosemary made her way home in quiet contemplation. Nothing seemed to have happened in the last few days in Myrtlewood, despite many of the Bermuda residents being around.

She'd seen them from time to time, dressed up in their hoity-toity clothes. A few of them had even come into the shop.

There had been enough relative peace and quiet in the town that Rosemary had almost let her guard down.

Aside from the night at the pub with Athena's birthday party, things couldn't have been smoother. Then again, the Lughnasa ritual was coming up next weekend and seasonal festivals always seemed to bring their own kind of magical chaos in Myrtlewood.

Rosemary arrived home to find another bouquet of roses on the doorstep. She carried it in, reading the note.

"From Burk? What has he done?" Athena asked, coming downstairs for the first time in a while.

Rosemary popped the bouquet on the kitchen counter. "You're out of your room."

"I got hungry," said Athena. "I already ate the snacks you left me, and despite my suggestions to the house there's still no kitchen in my bedroom." She set about making toast. "But I guess I can take this upstairs."

"Why don't you stay and talk to me for a while?" said Rosemary. "I don't like that you've been holed up in there, hiding under the covers."

"I'm only doing that part of the time," said Athena glumly. "I'm also painting."

"I'm glad you're still painting. It's good to have an outlet for all that fae energy."

"It's about the only thing I feel like I can do safely at the moment," said Athena. "I'm trying to avoid my magic...and my friends...and the town...and everything else."

Rosemary sighed. "Nobody has said anything about your party other than that it was a good time. I've told you. You didn't make a fool of yourself."

"Except what Elise saw..." Athena said. "She's probably told our other friends."

"Maybe she has," said Rosemary. "Sometimes people need to talk to someone."

"I won't have any friends left! They'll all take her side. They were her friends first. And I'll be a loner again."

"I'm sure it'll work out," said Rosemary.

"You haven't told me. What has Burk done?"

"Excuse me?"

"Why is he trying to apologise to you with a million bouquets of flowers every second day?"

Rosemary rolled her eyes. "I don't think he's done anything, exactly. I'm just a little bit confused."

Athena laughed. "Sorry, I don't mean to be rude. What's confusing? You like him, he likes you. Seems about perfect to me."

"It is just perfect, isn't it?"She frowned. "I just don't know if I can do relationships. It's too much to think about."

Athena sighed. "All I want is a committed relationship. And here you are with a perfectly nice vampire who's besotted with you. Plus, he's not going to go and die on you anytime soon or anything. And you like a him a lot. I can tell."

Rosemary folded her arms. "What's your point?"

"My point is you're scared of commitment," said Athena.

Rosemary felt the ring of truth. "Stop being so wise."

Athena took a bite of toast and smiled as if satisfied was herself. "I knew it. That's totally what's going on. Burk wants to have a proper relationship with you. And at the first sign of something being serious you've backed off and left him in the cold."

"I suppose you could put it like that," said Rosemary.

"It's just that you're scared. That's all," said Athena sagely. "That's the only thing that's going on here. You're scared and you're self-sabotaging. He's not getting clingy or anything is he?"

"No," said Rosemary. "He's been keeping a safe distance, I suspect."

"That's good." Athena took another bite of toast and a sip of the tea that Rosemary had just passed her.

"Why is it good?"

"That means he doesn't need you or anything."

"I suppose that is good. I don't think I could handle anyone needing me right now. Maybe we're better off being apart."

Athena laughed again. "Don't be ridiculous. The fact that he doesn't need you is good. But he's still clearly interested. That's exactly why you need to deal with your own insecurities."

"I have no idea how to do that." Rosemary stubbornly crossed her arms.

"You could start by talking to him," Athena suggested. "Tell him how you're feeling."

"Feelings..." said Rosemary. "Eww."

"Yep. I hear you," said Athena sympathetically. "But, you know sometimes you just need to grit your teeth and get on with it. Stop dragging it out. At any rate, if you don't like him break up with him."

"I can't break up with him," said Rosemary. "That's the point. We're not officially together."

Athena looked at her incredulously. "How would you feel if he started seeing someone else?"

Rosemary's gut tightened and she glared. "Who?!"

"Exactly," said Athena. "You are in a relationship even if you're in denial of it."

Rosemary sighed. "I'm finding this conversation uncomfortable."

"That's because it's important," said Athena. "Significant conversations often aren't comfortable."

"Stop being a wise arse," Rosemary grumbled.

"Hey," said Athena. "I'm in no position to be giving out romantic advice, am I? You just need to figure out what you really want. If it's not Burk, then you'd better tell him, and if it is, then well, you'd better tell him that as well."

"I suppose you're right. Just when I was thinking it might be easier to crawl under a rock for the rest of my life and avoid feelings."

"We'd all like that sometimes, wouldn't we?" said Athena. "Case in point." She gestured at herself.

"You seem better today actually."

"Maybe I'm slowly recovering."

"Do you think it was just the fae magic affecting you the other night? Are you feeling out of sorts at all?" Rosemary asked.

"No," said Athena. "Magic is quite frankly the easiest part of this. No, what I'm suffering from is terrible embarrassment. It's like a hangover. And my brain, it feels all heavy. It won't leave."

"Ah, the classic vulnerability hangover," said Rosemary. "Don't worry, love. It'll be gone soon enough." Rosemary gave her daughter a hug. "In the meantime, I suppose I have a certain vampire that I have to call."

Twenty-Nine

Rosemary had attempted to call Burk. Well, she'd got as far as staring at her phone anyway, and then she'd realised the situation was too complex for that.

"Athena is right," Rosemary muttered, putting on her boots and jacket. "It's unfair to leave him hanging."

She got into the car and began driving towards Burk's house with the sinking realisation that the decision was out of her control.

As much as she wanted Burk, Rosemary had long known that the relationship part of her was impossibly broken. She didn't want to play games. It wasn't fair to mess Burk around if he wanted something serious.

Athena had been right. Rosemary hated the thought of seeing Burk out with other women, but she had to admit to herself that her jealousy was inappropriate.

It was selfish of her not to let him see other people if, deep down, she knew she couldn't commit.

Rosemary pulled up outside the enormous castle that Burk called home, wishing she'd taken the cowards way out and left him a message instead.

"No," she told herself. "Don't be ridiculous. You owe him this much."

After her little pep talk she managed to drag herself up the steps to the grand entrance, and reached for the gargoyle door knocker.

Just as she touched it, the door creaked open.

An enormous hulking man was standing there.

"Uhh, hello?" said Rosemary. "I'm here to see Burk...Ahh, I suppose you're all Burks here. Err...Perseus?"

The man grunted and stood aside, gesturing for Rosemary to enter.

"I'm Rosemary Thorn," she said, taking a step inside. "And you are?"

The man just grunted again.

"A man of few words, I see," Rosemary muttered, looking around the entrance way. "Uhh, how do I find—"

"Who in Hades are you?" a young voice rang out. Rosemary looked to the top of the ornate staircase to see a girl of perhaps nine.

"Hello there," said Rosemary. "I'm just looking for Perseus. Is he around?"

The girl narrowed her eyes. "You didn't answer my question," she said, her tone giving away that she must have been older than she looked.

"My name's Rosemary Thorn."

The girl raised her eyebrows. "Am I supposed to be impressed by that?"

"Err...no?" said Rosemary. "I'm just he—"

"Oh, *Maman*, leave the poor thing alone," said Azalea, appearing from one of the dark hallways to Rosemary's right.

"Maman?" Rosemary asked, stunned. "This is your...?"

"Our matriarch, yes of course," said Azalea. "She's awfully grumpy after her nap, so don't let her get to you."

"What is this human doing in my house?" said the ancient girl.

"I'm sorry," said Rosemary, shock settling in her stomach like a weight. "I'm just adjusting. I'm here to see Burk, uhh, Perseus... only. Well, you look so young. I guess it's not that different to Geneviève, really."

The 'girl' glared daggers at Rosemary. "Do not mention that name in my house!"

"Uhh, okay. Sorry," said Rosemary. "If it's any consolation I'm not a fan of her either. In fact, she's on the list of my least favourite people...uhh...vampires—not that I'm prejudiced against your kind, err...I'll stop now."

There was a moment of awkward silence before Azalea threw back her head and cried, "Fascinating!"

"What's that, dear?" said a man's voice. Rosemary turned to her left to see someone who looked rather out of place. The man was tall, muscular, and blonde, and was clad in a white tennis outfit complete with sweat bands and a racket. He strolled over to stand next to Azalea, giving her a peck on the cheek.

"This must be Percy's new flame," said the man.

Percy! Rosemary had to stop herself from laughing as he introduced himself.

"Hi, I'm Chuck."

"Chuck?" Rosemary asked as she shook the man's hand, still getting used to the sight of the odd pair in front of her.

Azalea crowed with laughter. "Oh don't mind him," she said. "He goes through these phases, don't you, Charles? I know it's gauche, but it's also amusingly ironic, the personalities he comes up with. It certainly keeps things interesting over the centuries... especially in the boudoir."

Rosemary felt her eyes bulge in surprise. "I'll take your word for it," she said.

"Stop tolerating the filthy human," said Azalea's tiny mother.

"Dora," said Charles. "Come now, we must be gracious hosts of Percy's lady friend."

"Err, speaking of—"

Rosemary was interrupted by a scrambling noise and a strange creature scuttled into view. At first she assumed it was some kind of mythical beast she'd never seen before, but after a moment she realised the figure was humanoid, just with an odd, crablike way of moving about and long, wild, matted black hair.

"Don't mind Byron," said Azalea. "He doesn't come out of the crypt often. He's intrigued by fleshies."

"Fleshies?" Rosemary asked. "Oh..." She folded her arms and pinched the skin on her forearm. "I guess I am rather fleshy," she admitted. Compared to Burk's firm sculpted muscle, anyway.

Byron came uncomfortably close to her, grunted, and sniffed.

Rosemary wondered if he was non-verbal until he screeched, "She killed him!"

"W—what?" Rosemary stuttered, feeling a sudden flood of fear.

"Cyrus," said Azalea, "our poor lost lamb." She clutched her heart.

Rosemary balked. She had indeed killed Burk's wayward brother, though it had clearly been in self-defence before she knew who he was.

"Uhh..." Rosemary couldn't find the right words and doubted there were any. She began slowly backing towards the door.

"Byron is psychic, you know," Charles remarked coolly. "It's all in the scent."

By this time, Dora had made her way down the steps. She, Charles, and Azalea were staring at Rosemary, edging closer.

Rosemary took several more steps back but bumped into something. It was the large hulking doorman, who grunted.

"I'll just go," said Rosemary. "Yes, actually. I think I left something in the oven."

"How?" Azalea asked.

Byron skuttled back again and took another sniff. "A stake through the heart!" he cried.

Rosemary's heart was racing. She had the very strong urge to run away as quickly as possible, but feared it would be impossible.

Azalea's face spread into a slightly maniacal smile. "I told you she was fascinating," she said, taking a step back.

"Impressive," said Charles.

"Who would have thought one so weak would be capable..." Dora muttered.

"Oh, stop it, Pandora," said Charles. "You'll offend our guest."

"Yes, *Maman*, please behave yourself," said Azalea.

Rosemary took a deep breath. "You're not mad?" she asked incredulously.

"It was a tragedy," Azalea said theatrically, with her hand on her heart.

"But then again, his whole life was," said Charles.

Pandora chuckled. "He's gone to Hades now, where he belongs."

"But," said Azalea, "the penalty must be paid."

"Penalty?" Rosemary asked, with a gulp.

"Of course," said Azalea, reaching out towards Rosemary's head. "Life for life."

Rosemary flinched and jumped back.

"Couldn't I just give you some chocolates or something? I know vampires don't exactly eat, but Marjie could blood-enchant them, they're really very good..." she began rambling.

"Azzy, you're scaring the poor girl," said Charles.

"Oh, forgive me," said Azalea. "I don't mean to kill you..."

"You don't?" said Rosemary. "Well, thank goodness for that."

"What my darling was trying so say," Charles continued, "is welcome to the family!"

"You can't escape now," Byron chucked.

They beamed at her, all of them except for Pandora, who scowled. Rosemary was stunned. "Err..."

"You're one of us now," said Azalea. "And we always protect our own."

Rosemary gulped, not wanting to let them down with the

fact that she'd arrived to break it off with their son...or grandson, or whatever relationship he was to Byron.

"That's very...err,"—she avoided the word nice—"...generous of you. But I'm really just here to see..."

"Perseus, of course," said Azalea. "He's just in his coffin."

"Coffin, of course," said Rosemary.

"It's a figure of speech," said Charles, with a jaunty smile. "Can we offer you some refreshments?"

"Ooh yes." Azalea clapped her hands. "I have a selection of pickled organ meats."

"What's going on here?"

Rosemary turned, relieved to see Burk.

"Rosemary? This is a surprise. They haven't scared you off, have they?"

"Uhh," Rosemary started.

"*Mother*?" Burk said, a warning in his voice.

"We were just getting to know her," said Azalea defensively.

"Come," said Burk. He took Rosemary's hand, and before she knew it she was whisked away into the tower room where they'd had their romantic dinner.

Rosemary melted as the very attractive vampire kissed her, taking her breath away.

"Burk," she said. "I need to talk to—"

But Burk closed the door to the tower, then pushed her up against it, kissing her again. "Don't," he said, placing a kiss down her neck in between each word. "listen—to—a—single—word—they—say."

"It's not that," said Rosemary, although her body was responding rather rapidly to his touch, and her mind was becoming vague, even though she was sure she had something very serious to discuss.

Get a grip, she told herself, and pushed Burk away.

He looked at her questioningly.

"There's something important I want to discuss," she said.

"Can it wait?" Burk asked. "Because I had rather wanted to ravage you with pleasure this instant."

"I don't think it would be fair to you..." said Rosemary.

"At this point," said Burk, "it's taking all my energy to hold back, so unless you're unwilling..."

"It's not that," Rosemary said.

"I don't think it would be fair to me...or perhaps to both of us...if we have to delay."

"You have a point," said Rosemary, letting go of her inhibitions and pulling Burk in for another kiss. "But..." she said as she pulled back again.

"Do you want this?" Burk asked.

"Yes," Rosemary admitted.

"Then relax," said Burk. "Whatever it is you have to tell me can wait, at least a few moments...or hours."

Rosemary lay in Burk's soft, luxurious bed approximately two hours later feeling terribly guilty.

She groaned.

"Did I hurt you?" he asked, concerned.

"No, it's not that. Well, only in a good way."

He grinned at her. "Then why the long face?"

Rosemary sighed. "To be quite frank, I came over here because, well, I know you want commitment, and I can't give it to you. And Athena told me I should make up my mind and stop stringing you along."

"Is that what you're doing?" he asked in a nonchalant fashion. "Are you trying to string me along, here?" He narrowed his eyes and smiled charmingly. "You're playing with me, Rosemary Thorn."

"Of course not," said Rosemary. "Not intentionally."

"Look, I'm sorry if I came on too strong. I never meant to give you an ultimatum. I'm happy just being in your presence."

"Are you, though?" Rosemary asked. "You said you didn't want anything casual."

Burk shook his head. "It's not like that. I don't tend to do casual flings, that's true, but that doesn't mean I'm demanding anything of you in particular. What I want is to be with you. And if you don't want any kind of boring, serious, old fashioned commitment, then I suppose I can live with it." He grinned.

"That's the thing," said Rosemary. "I'm not particularly good at casual either. In fact, I think I'd get quite jealous if you were seeing other people."

"I'm not interested in seeing other people," said Burk with a serious tone.

"Maybe you can find someone to be seriously committed to though." Rosemary gritted her teeth. "It would make me jealous. But that's just selfish of me. If that's what you want you should date other people and find someone who wants the same things."

Burk laughed.

"What?" Rosemary asked.

He leaned back, stretching his arms behind his head. "Maybe I will, one day," he said. "But I'm not interested in dating anyone else, and even if you choose to break it off now I probably wouldn't be. Not for a few hundred years, anyway."

"That's oddly romantic," said Rosemary, leaning her head on his chest. "But seriously. Don't be ridiculous."

"I'm not. I just...I don't fall in love easily, Rosemary."

"You're in love?"

"I am. I didn't want to scare you off by telling you, but I suppose I've somehow driven you away anyway."

"No, it's not you."

He laughed. "You're not one for such cliches."

"I mean it, I'm broken."

"Broken or scared?"

"Both."

"Well, then, why can't we be broken and scared together?"

"That also sounds kind of romantic, in a sad way," said Rosemary.

"Tell me," said Burk. "What is that you really want? I know you're scared. Then again, life is full of terrifying things. So if you put that aside..."

Rosemary buried her face into Burk's sculpted chest and groaned. "I want you," she mumbled.

"What was that?" Burk asked, tickling her gently.

"I want you, silly – stop that."

"Well, if that's the case, I'm all yours," he said. "For as long as you'll have me."

"But I can't commit," said Rosemary.

"To what?" Burk asked. "Do you want to be polyamorous,

now? Because I can't say I'm entirely on-board with that, but I'd give it a try if you're interested."

"Goddess no," said Rosemary. "Not being judgemental or anything. I can barely handle any relationship at all, let alone multiple!"

"I'm not asking you to marry me or anything. Just enjoy my company for however long it may last."

Rosemary rolled onto her back and folded her arms. She looked at the incredibly attractive vampire who lay next to her. "I suppose I could do that," she said.

"Good," said Burk. "I promised to make it worth your while." With a cheeky grin, he kissed her again.

"I suppose it's just as well we're not breaking it off," said Rosemary. "Your mother might disapprove."

"Why do you say that?"

"Apparently, I'm part of the family, now."

Burk looked at her, astonished. "Why, Rosemary Thorn," he said. "You never fail to amaze me."

Thirty

"You're all dressed up," Rosemary said as Athena entered the kitchen.

"And you're still in your dressing gown," said Athena.

"So I am."

Rosemary smiled at her daughter and handed her the cup of tea she'd been about to take upstairs for her. It was the first time Athena looked to be getting ready to go out. "Where are you off to, then?" she asked.

"To the Lughnasa festival, of course," said Athena, taking a sip. "Aren't you coming?"

Rosemary frowned. "I thought I might give it a miss, actually," she said. "The last thing we need is more drama."

"That might be the case," said Athena. "But I suspect something sketchy is going to happen and if we're not there we won't be able to work out what it is. More to the point, we won't be able to stop it. This is our town and we have to protect it."

Rosemary sighed. "I suppose you're right, though there are plenty of magical people around town, especially right now with all the Bermuda evacuees."

"I'm sure something suspicious is brewing," said Athena. "And I'm far too curious to stay home."

Rosemary smiled. "Well, it's nice to see you up and about. Pancakes?" She held up a plate.

"Excellent!" said Athena. "I'll eat while you get dressed."

Myrtlewood town was unusually crowded as they arrived near the centre.

"Just what I wanted to do on my day off," said Rosemary. "Go and hang out with a bunch of magical snobs in a situation that's bound to be dangerous."

Athena laughed. "Oh come on," she said. "It's not like you even know how to rest and relax properly, anyway."

"I don't know," said Rosemary. "Maybe if I had a hammock..."

"Tell you what. After we've dealt with whatever this particular form of magical mayhem is, I'll buy you one as a present."

"Really?" said Rosemary, sounding particularly excited.

"Sure," said Athena. "Even though you're rich enough to buy yourself one."

"Yeah, but it's not the same if it's not a gift."

They wandered towards the crowd gathered in the circle in the middle of town. It was a much larger gathering than usual.

Rosemary thought she recognized a few of the gathered attendees from the fancy event in Bermuda. She stared at them suspiciously.

"Stop doing that," Athena said.

"What? I'm just scoping things out."

"Yeah, but if you keep staring at people like that, everyone's going to be suspicious of us."

"All right," said Rosemary.

"Maybe we should leave the snooping to the professionals."

"Hey, look, somebody's walking in. Is that Ferg?" Rosemary asked as a hooded figure entered the circle.

"I don't think so," said Athena.

The figure pulled back their hood to reveal a black and silver striped bob and horn rimmed spectacles.

"It's the Arch Magistrate!" Rosemary whispered.

"I can see that," said Athena. "I have eyes."

Ferg joined her in the centre and the crowd hushed.

"Myrtlewood townspeople," he said with grandiosity. "For this very special Lughnasa festival we have an honoured guest officiating for us. May I introduce, the Arch Magistrate, herself."

The Arch Magistrate bowed and the audience applauded.

Then a bell rang and the ceremony began and the crowd hushed.

The Arch Magistrate spoke of the families and communities coming together, growing of fields of grain, the harvest, the baking of bread.

"Golly, she goes on lot doesn't she?" Rosemary whispered to Athena.

"I thought you liked her," Athena said.

"I'm just saying..." Rosemary continued quietly. "Just because somebody is a great bureaucrat doesn't mean they're a great public speaker, does it?"

"Quiet. I'm trying to listen. There might be a clue."

The ritual went into full swing. The quarters were called in a fairly usual way, except the callers happened to be some of the posh witching people from Bermuda, including none other than Rosemary's own uncle Ernest, summoning fire.

"Of course he's summoning fire," Athena said.

"No surprises there, I guess," said Rosemary. "Elamina said her gift with fire comes from her father's side. Very suspicious," she muttered.

"No, it isn't," said Athena. "We haven't had much with fire recently at all."

"Explosions are pretty similar to fire though, aren't they? Maybe it's disguised somehow," said Rosemary, though she wasn't particularly convinced, herself.

"You can make explosions too," Athena muttered. "I'm surprised you haven't blown up the whole house. I can't say the same for the poor greenhouse. It's lucky Thorn Manor can restore itself."

Next came a ceremonial sharing of bread and honey around the circle. Small pieces of bread were distributed by other unfamiliar witches, while others passed around bowls of honey to dip the bread into.

"Now, as you savour this delicacy of the season," the Arch

Magistrate said, "close your eyes and feel the ripening fruit of the harvest, both real and metaphorical in your lives."

Rosemary did not close her eyes, just in case. But, with the taste of honey and freshly baked bread, there did come a sense of abundance.

"Now open your eyes," the Arch Magistrate ordered. "And witness the magic of Lughnasa."

The crowd gasped in wonder as golden light appeared in the centre of the circle, shaping itself into an orb that sprouted and grew into an enormous wheat plant. It shifted again into an entire field of grain that they were now part of.

Rosemary could feel the warm sun shining down on her. It was almost as if she was a plant growing towards the nourishment of the light.

The light transformed again into the wheat being hulled and then milled into flour and baked into bread ready to be shared by families and communities.

Rosemary felt the magic of Lughnasa emanating around the circle – the power of the magical rite. It was subtle and warm – harvest magic. She breathed it in, feeling a kind of culmination in her own life.

The chocolate shop was running smoothly. And aside from a few hiccups with Athena and magical politics, everything did indeed seem to be coming to a point of fruition.

She smiled in satisfaction as she savoured the last remnants of flavour.

"In honour of the Sun god, Lugh..." said the Arch Magistrate.

"Honouring's fine," Rosemary whispered to Athena. "As long as we're not summoning him or anything."

Athena elbowed her again. "Behave yourself, Mother."

Rosemary sighed and the Arch Magistrate shot her an odd look.

I told you, you'll get us into trouble, Athena said in Rosemary's mind. *Okay?*

"Okay, I'll behave," Rosemary whispered.

The Arch Magistrate continued to stare at Rosemary for a long moment and then continued on with the proceedings. "I proclaim this festival of Lughnasa complete."

Thirty-One

"Well, that was a rather uneventful festival," said Athena.

"Delightfully so." Rosemary smiled as the ritual wound to a close. "Wait a minute."

"What?" Athena asked.

"Look over there."

"Is that Beryl's parents?"

"Yes, talking to each other in a way that looks rather suspicious."

"Oh, come off it."

"Seriously," said Rosemary. "I have an instinct for these things even if you don't believe it. I'm going to follow them."

"Don't be ridiculous," said Athena.

"Come on. We're grasping at straws here, but I'm sure they have something to do with this."

They followed the Flarguans, who got into an expensive

black car parked just a few spaces up from the Thorn Rolls Royce.

"Don't you think it'll be rather ostentatious following them in this beast of a vehicle?" Athena asked.

"Beautiful beast," said Rosemary defensively. "Don't worry. We'll keep a safe distance. And whatever happens you stay in the car."

"I don't get it," said Athena. "Earlier today you wanted to stay home to avoid drama and now you're deliberately wading into it neck deep."

Rosemary shook her head. "I'd love to be able to avoid it, but I have a feeling that if we don't get to the bottom of this it will all come crashing down on us. I have to trust my gut."

Athena sighed. "Whatever," she said, following her mother into the vehicle.

They drove a respectful distance from the black Mercedes the Flarguans were being chauffeured in. Rosemary slowed when it pulled into a driveway with high fences and an elaborate gate which closed automatically behind them.

Rosemary waited a moment and then drove past, slowly looking in. "It's not going to be easy," she said to Athena.

"What isn't?"

"Going in there," Rosemary said, pulling up the car further down the road.

"Wait a minute," said Athena. "You're not seriously—"

"Wait here," said Rosemary. She got out and scoped out the property, convinced that there must be some way to get closer to the house and find out more. Sure enough, there was a wooded area around a bit connected to the property next door.

Rosemary looked both ways before slipping down the neighbour's pathway and made her way behind the house to the wood. She stumbled through the trees in the general direction of the Farguan's mansion and quietly made her way through several ornamental gardens complete with Romanesque statues before reaching the back entrance, which was larger and more elaborate than most of the front doors she'd ever encountered.

Just as she neared the back door she heard a shout.

"Hey! Excuse me, what are you doing here?"

Rosemary spotted black clad figures that looked to be some sort of guards. She'd kept her eyes peeled for protective spells but hadn't expected actual security workers.

She started running back towards the forest, reaching it moments later. She sprinted through the trees, her heart racing, only allowing herself to relax after she'd reached the car and she seemed to have lost them.

"What was all that about?" Athena asked.

"They've got security."

"Can you blame them with people like you snooping around?"

"Oh, stop that," said Rosemary.

"Can we go home now?" Athena pleaded.

"Yes, I think we'll have to. I need to work out how I can conceal myself and sneak back in."

Athena sighed dramatically as Rosemary started the car and began to drive back towards Thorn Manor.

"I'm not sure about this hare-brained scheme," said Neve as Rosemary prepared the concealment spell in the lounge of Thorn Manor.

"Well, who has the luxury of being sure of anything?" said Rosemary. "Anyway, I didn't call you over here for you to give me a vote of confidence. I just wanted you to know what was going on because...well, you're the law enforcement around here and I thought it was the responsible thing to do. Besides, you're a good friend and I wanted someone else to know in case anything happens to me."

"It makes it even worse when you put it like that," said Neve.

"Are you going to stop me?" Rosemary asked.

Neve folded her arms and pressed her lips together. "Have you got enough for two in this concealment spell?"

Rosemary grinned. "I knew there was a reason we're friends. I suppose I do."

"I figure if my good friend is doing something utterly erratic, I'd better come with you."

"Well, I don't know if the spell is going to work," Rosemary warned. "And Nesta will never forgive me if anything happens to you."

Neve gave her pointed look.

"Oh very well," said Rosemary. "If you insist. Athena thinks I'm bonkers, which is really just as well," Rosemary continued. "I'd rather her not try to come along. Those Flarguans are nasty and I don't think they'd take kindly to my fae-witch daughter showing up at their house. They probably discriminate against 'half-breeds'."

Neve gave her a disgusted look.

"Exactly my point," said Rosemary. "In fact, they don't like any other species there. They've self-identified as witch supremacists."

"I've never heard that term before," said Neve, with a shrug. "They don't exactly sound like great people."

"Which is exactly why I need to figure out what's going on," said Rosemary.

"If they're so magical," said Neve, "surely they have a whole lot of protections over their house."

"I had a look, earlier. Either they've hidden their protections well or...actually I'm kind of counting on them being so arrogant that they haven't done a proper job with their magical security system. You know, thinking that nobody's as clever as they are?"

Neve shrugged. "I hope you're right."

"Either way, everyone keeps telling me the Thorn magic is so strong and powerful. If this is true we should have an advantage, surely."

Rosemary finished preparing the ingredients for the concealment spell. Then she grabbed hold a handful of quartz crystals before passing them to Neve.

"Okay, stand back. No. To the left." Rosemary positioned Neve around the circle of lavender she'd placed on the floor. "All right. Close your eyes. I'm just going to weave us a little web."

It wasn't the easiest thing to do, holding onto quartz crystals while moving her fingers around in a complicated way. Rosemary made do with two of her five fingers on each hand and her thumb. Sure enough, the magic seemed to be working. Little threads of light appeared from her fingertips then wove themselves in the air around her and the detective. She carried on moving her fingers in concentration until the web covered them both.

"Alright," said Rosemary. "You can open your eyes now."

"Is it done?" Neve asked as little waves of light faded into her skin.

Rosemary nodded. "Did you feel anything?"

"Just a sort of tingling."

"Well, if it has worked, it should last us a couple of hours."

"But I can still see myself, and you…"

Rosemary laughed. "It would be much more confusing if we couldn't see each other. Let's test it. Athena!" she called out.

"Mum?" Athena ran into the lounge. "Where are you?"

"Right here," said Rosemary.

"Oh my goodness. It actually worked!" said Athena in an astonished voice. "I can't see you at all. Where exactly are you?"

"Just by the circle," said Rosemary.

Athena came over, waving her hands in the air until she found Rosemary's shoulder. "You're still solid."

"I should hope so," said Rosemary. "But that is a good point to consider. I don't think the spell will protect our bodies. It'll just make us hard to see for a while. I'm hoping that'll be enough to get us in."

"It's a pretty cool magical disguise," said Athena, staring into the air where Rosemary and Neve stood.

Rosemary looked at her daughter. It was an odd feeling to know Athena couldn't see her. "I hope you don't mind, but I'm borrowing some of your charms and potion arsenal for Neve to use."

"Go ahead," said Athena. "I need to make more anyway."

"I suppose that's another creative outlet," said Rosemary.

Athena looked unimpressed. "Just don't do anything stupid," she said, staring slightly away from where Rosemary's face was. "I'm counting on you coming back to be my mother and continuing to boss me around."

"Okay. Okay," Rosemary said as she kissed her rather startled daughter on the cheek. And then she and Neve prepared to leave the house, getting into Neve's undercover car with its conveniently tinted windows, and made their way to Flarguan mansion.

Thirty-Two

Rosemary led Neve to the back entrance, down the neighbour's path, and through the forest.

"The door's open," said Neve, pointing up ahead.

"Strange," Rosemary whispered as they approached. "I don't see any signs of security guards either."

Neve cleared her throat. "You mean, like those guys in black clothes?"

"Where?"

"Lying on the ground," Neve replied, pointing out the figures strewn about.

"Oh Goddess," said Rosemary. "Are they dead?"

Neve reached the nearest security guard and checked his pulse. "No, just out cold, I think. Probably magic."

"What on earth..."

"Ahh, Rosemary?"

"Yes?"

"I think your veiling charm is wearing off."

Rosemary looked to see that Neve was right. The previously invisible web was reappearing, fraying as it disintegrated.

"Drat! There must be magical protections on the house, after all. Let's hurry and figure out what's going on."

They dashed through the mansion, noting the chaos. Shards of glass and pottery littered the floor, as if cabinets and expensive vases had been carelessly flung around. Antique furniture lay at odd angles, some of it broken.

"What caused all this?" Rosemary asked. "Do you think the Flarguans lost control of their magic?"

"I don't think so," Neve replied. "Look."

She pulled Rosemary into an old fashioned drawing room. It could have been out of a museum, nothing modern in sight. Unlike the rest of the house, this room was perfectly orderly except for two figures, tied up elaborately in what looked like vines, which were hanging from the ceiling.

Neve stepped cautiously towards them while Rosemary held back.

"Are they..."

"They're breathing," said Neve. "But unconscious."

"So it wasn't them," said Rosemary. "I was so sure they were up to something. That'll teach me to trust my gut."

"Look!" said Neve, pointing to a bright purple feather lying on the ground underneath the Flarguans, who were just starting to stir.

"The calling card of the Countess of West Eloria," said Rosemary. "Maybe it is her, after all...I thought it was too obvious."

"You said she can't have been behind the magical explosions in Bermuda."

"Dain said fae magic can't do that sort of combustion, but perhaps she's found a way. Either that, or someone else is setting her up and we're back to square one. What do you think happened here?"

"What is the meaning of this?" said an authoritative voice.

Rosemary turned towards the door to see none other than the Arch Magistrate herself, walking into the room.

"Why are you here?" Rosemary asked, before she could censor her own mind.

The Magistrate glared at her over her horn rimmed spectacles. "*I* am staying here," she said. "I was at the Bracewell-Thorn's Lughnasa soirée. I just popped back to pick up a book I wanted to lend to Derse...Now tell me, what is the meaning of this?!"

She gestured around the house and then to the Flarguans, who were now looking around, as if in a daze.

"I...umm," Rosemary started.

"These miscreants are breaking and entering," said Cecily Flarguan in a shrill voice, as if just beginning to take in the situation. "The house is a mess!"

"And we seem to be restrained," Ernest added, sounding irritated.

Neve flashed her police badge around the room. "We're investigating a situation," she said simply.

Rosemary was not quite so concise. She couldn't help rambling. "Yes...we were just. Err... investigating...and stumbled across all this. Honestly! Neve's a detective..."

"And you?" the Magistrate asked pointedly.

"I'm just helping out," said Rosemary, though her tone sounded unconvincing, even to her.

"Rosemary is a part-time consultant for the Myrtlewood police authorities," said Neve, in a much more confident tone.

"Alright then," said the Magistrate. "Would you care to explain what in Cerridwen's name is going on?"

"What happened?" Neve asked Cecily and Ernest. "How did the house get like this? Who tied you up?"

"It's funny," said Ernest. "I don't seem to recall anything past morning tea today."

"Someone has befuddled us!" Cecily cried.

The Arch Magistrate looked at them all in disbelief as Rosemary bumbled her way through her theory about the countess, and the previous incidents involving mysterious purple feathers. After a moment of silence, she spoke. "You're saying a high fae countess is behind all this?"

"Savages! Miscreants!" Cecily shouted. "Get out of my house with your foul faery associates!"

"Now, now, Cecily," said Ernest Flarguan awkwardly. "Let the Magistrate do her job."

"Yes," said Rosemary. "It's probably the countess, or someone else pretending to be her...but we don't know who."

"Nonsense," said the Magistrate. "How would she even get through the veil? The protections are immense."

"That's what we're trying to work out," said Rosemary. "In the past she's sent servants through."

"Servants?"

"There was...a local boy, with a fae mother and human father."

"Disgusting!" Cecily cried. The Magistrate shot her a look that silenced her immediately.

*Finnigan...*Rosemary thought. *He said he had nothing more to do with the countess...that he just happened to find that feather... he's played us for fools and he just happens to be staying with Athena's dad!*

Rosemary's heart fluttered in anxiety. She had to warn Dain of the possible danger.

Thirty-Three

Athena paced her bedroom.

Things were not normal. Not at all. And to top it all off she was worried about Rosemary, who had been only been gone for ten minutes.

Ten minutes is a lot of time when it comes to my mother getting herself into trouble.

Athena would have gone with Rosemary, if only to try and protect her from getting into too much of a mess, however she was in no fit state.

Her whole body was tingling, as if she was covered in thousands of tiny magical fires. It wasn't pain exactly. It almost felt good, except for the fact that it was so disconcerting. She didn't want to worry Rosemary with another fae magical drama. Besides, Athena wanted to be alone. The last thing she needed was to be fussed over.

Her eyes fell on her canvasses. Rosemary had bought her a

whole pile of new ones, along with extra art supplies for her birthday.

Maybe this will help, Athena thought, setting up a fresh canvas. She selected paints at random again. She didn't have the attention span to try to paint anything in particular, so instead she just tried mindless painting again, allowing herself to zone out while swirling greens and blues, purples and pinks, whites and yellows, losing herself in the artform in a kind of flow that seemed to take over her body. She quickly finished with the first canvas and started a second, and then a third.

As she painted, she had a strange sensation that her art was alive. Even the drying canvases seemed, out of the corner of her eye, to become three dimensional, almost like vortexes into other worlds.

Athena felt herself drawn into them, floating, soaring, flying through these other worlds in her mind as she continued to paint.

There was a sensation of breeze against her skin. It flowed all around the room, though the windows remained closed. Athena felt as if she was being swept up into something far bigger than just herself, as the whole room began to swim.

Thirty-Four

"I'm afraid I may have to detain you," the Arch Magistrate said to Rosemary. "The chaos in this house might not have been caused by you, but the situation is too suspicious. This is simply unacceptable. Besides, you've broken into the Flarguan house."

"Rosemary isn't under your jurisdiction," said Neve.

"She's a witch!" said the Arch Magistrate sharply.

"Yes, but you have no proof that she's using magic irresponsibly. Any tests you run here won't bear her magical signature and will show she's innocent. Breaking and entering, on the other hand, is a matter for local law enforcement, and as I said, she was helping me."

"Where is your warrant?" Ernest cried.

Neve smiled politely. "In Myrtlewood we have a section 7AA of the Magical Malevolence Regulations—an officer is allowed to enter a property if they deem there are significant enough risks." Neve gestured around. "Clearly there are."

Rosemary chuckled nervously and leaned against the mantle-piece. Her finger caught on a little button and she couldn't help but push it. A golden scroll case appeared with a little pop on the drawing room table, and unrolled itself.

"Well, what do we have here?" Neve asked.

"That's private!" Ernest bellowed. "Don't look."

But it was too late. Rosemary, Neve and the Arch Mage had already crowded around in curiosity.

The scroll was covered in loopy old-fashioned writing that Rosemary struggled to decipher, though she easily recognised the technical drawings of the village of Myrtlewood and what appeared to be the Bermuda complex.

"These are plans to sabotage the treaty," the Arch Magistrate said in a very serious tone.

"No they aren't," said Cecily primly, while at the same time Ernest screeched out, "All hypothetical! Nothing to see here."

The Arch Magistrate raised her eyebrows. "I'm afraid this isn't nothing," she said. "It's strong evidence of treason."

"We haven't done a thing," said Cecily.

"Purely speculation!," Ernest added. "You'll see that nothing written there has been carried out, not a jot!"

"He's right," said Neve. "This involves a lot of magical possibilities, potions and enchantments, even mind-control, but no explosions or anything."

"Still, it's treacherous," said the Arch Magistrate. "We cannot tolerate it. You must both stand trial, along with any accomplices. There will be consequences."

Cecily looked stunned, while Ernest seemed resigned.

Neve began telling Ernest and Cecily their rights, which were slightly different from any crime shows Rosemary had watched, including a right to magical counsel. She placed a silver tracking bracelet around their left wrists. It seemed they had a day to get their affairs in order before the magical authorities would transport them to Glastonbury to await trial.

After all this, Neve untied the Flarguans, who were still protesting wildly.

Rosemary felt little sympathy for them, as bigoted and mean as they seemed to be.

"Walk me out," the Arch Magistrate said.

It was more of a command than a request. Neve and Rosemary looked at each other, then followed her out of the mansion.

"After all that, I think I need a cup of tea!" the Arch Magistrate announced.

"You're welcome to pop around to our place," Rosemary reminded her.

"I can't wait." She pulled a little bejewelled purple and gold box out of her handbag and tapped it three times with her little finger.

The box floated in mid-air and then sprouted legs and grew into a table. It landed gently on the Flarguans' front lawn, with matching chairs and a fully equipped tea tray, complete with a steaming purple and gold teapot and three matching cups.

"I need one of these in my life!" Rosemary exclaimed.

The Arch Magistrate gestured for them to sit and poured them all tea. "An unexpected development, indeed," she said. "Tell me, detective, exactly what do you think is going on here?"

Rosemary had just taken a sip of tea when there was a little pop and Reginald appeared next to them on the lawn. He handed the Arch Magistrate a scroll and then looked around in horror. "What is the meaning of this?!"

The Arch Magistrate raised her finger for quiet as she read the note.

"Err...looks like you're busy. We'd better get going," said Rosemary.

"Not so fast," the Magistrate replied. "I'm sorry," she said, looking at Rosemary.

"Sorry for what?"

"Rosemary Thorn, you are hereby under detention. You have twenty-seven hours to get your affairs in order before standing trial."

Neve's jaw dropped as Reginald snapped a little silver bracelet over Rosemary's wrist, similar to the one placed on the Flarguans only minutes before.

"But..." Rosemary looked around in shock. "Why?"

"The magical residue tests have finally come back from Bermuda. A clear signature was identified from the explosions. It was your magic."

"That's impossible!" said Rosemary. "It was nothing to do with me."

"Save your defence for the trial," said Reginald. "And don't try to run or hide. Wherever in this world you are, we will find you."

Neve dropped Rosemary off outside Thorn Manor. She looked up at the house in the late afternoon light. She couldn't believe the day still wasn't over yet, but then again, the Lughnasa ritual had been a morning one. Still, it seemed like a lifetime ago.

Despite the slow passage of time, she wasn't quite ready to face Athena yet.

Athena had warned her not to go, had told Rosemary it would only lead to trouble.

Athena had been right.

And now how was Rosemary supposed to explain to her newly seventeen-year-old that her mother was going to stand trial for explosions she clearly had nothing to do with...but that still might lead to her imprisonment?

Rosemary sighed.

Instead of going into the house, she got into the car and began to drive. She needed a moment or two to think before having to explain herself.

She was clearly being framed, but if not by the Flarguans, then by whom?

The countess was the obvious suspect, but she couldn't get into the Earth realm alone. Someone had to be helping her, but having the power to travel between the realms was rare.

*Finnigan...*Rosemary recalled. *He's done it before, so many times! He can travel between the realms easily and he's worked for the countess before. Of course he's the most likely suspect!*

She turned the car around and drove directly to Dain's apartment where she knew the wayward fae boy had been staying. Dain had naïvely taken a liking to him, but clearly that was a mistake...*Unless Dain is in on it too!* Rosemary had been surprised at how quick his journey to the fae realm had been. Was it possible that he'd turned traitor? Or perhaps he was being coerced by the countess, somehow. She tried to push her intense suspicions from her mind. Dain had turned over a new leaf and was actually finding some stability for once in his life. There was no way he'd throw it all away, and he'd be a tough personality to manipulate – as infuriating as he was!

Rosemary now trusted Dain – after all these years. It was an unexpected insight that left her more puzzled than anything.

She definitely did not trust Finnigan, however. That was clear.

Rosemary had never been in to the apartment before, but she knew which building it was in, above Mervin's ice cream parlour. Thankfully, there were names listed by the buzzers.

Rosemary pressed the one next to Dain's. Number 3.

"Hello?" Dain's voice came through the speaker, and Rosemary felt a sense of relief.

"Uhh, hi."

"Rosemary? This is a surprise. Come on up."

The door swung open and Rosemary climbed the steps and tentatively pushed open the door to number three, which had been left slightly ajar.

"And to what do I owe this honour?" Dain's voice called down the hallway. Rosemary entered a small open plan living and dining area, surprised to find it clean and tidy, and even more surprised to find both Dain and Finnigan sitting around the table, holding small blocks of wood and chisels.

"Err?" said Rosemary.

"Whittling," said Dain. "It's a fae past time." He picked something up from the table and handed it to her. It was a tiny wooden boar, expertly carved.

"You used to make me this kind of thing," Rosemary recalled. "When we first got together."

Dain nodded.

Finnigan smiled at her and then returned his attention to his whittling.

Rosemary felt uncertain, all of a sudden. She'd come to warn Dain, to confront Finnigan...but he seemed to look so young and innocent there with his tiny chisel and small piece of pine.

"What is it?" Dain asked. "Is something wrong with Athena?"

"No...I mean, just the same stuff, I think, but well..."

"She came because of me," said Finnigan.

"Oi!" said Rosemary. "Out of my head."

"It's Leithrein, isn't it?" Finnigan continued.

Rosemary sighed and explained the recent events.

"Impossible," said Dain. "There was no way you could have pulled of anything as epic as those explosions."

"Tell that to the judge," said Rosemary. "Which I assume will be the Arch Magistrate. She's very unimpressed with me, which is a shame really, seeing as we got off to such a good start."

"You might not believe me," said Finnigan, "but I'm totally innocent in all of this. I earned my freedom from Leithrein and never looked back. I've barely even dared return to the realm in case I get captured and enslaved again. Not worth it."

"He's telling the truth," said Dain.

"How can you be so sure?" Rosemary asked.

"Condition of him staying here," said explained. "He had to open up his mind to me. I know basically everything there is to know about the boy – whether I like it or not."

Rosemary looked at him, slightly mortified.

"Don't worry," Dain added. "He barely even kissed Athena."

Rosemary looked between them. "How do you know it isn't some kind of trick?"

Dain shrugged. "I'm immune to the charms of other fae. Is it really so hard for you to imagine that the boy is turning over a new leaf?"

Rosemary sighed. "I suppose not," she said. "But it leaves us with no leads."

"You're right about one thing," Finnigan said. "Leithrein will need help to get through. Not only that, she'll likely be coming in where the veil is weakest."

"Finn's Creek?" Rosemary asked. "That's what I was thinking."

"My creek," said Finnigan. "I'm not certain, but I like to think it was named after me...you know, seeing as I disappeared there all those years ago."

Dain reached over and patted him on the shoulder in a fatherly way.

"Well, that's something," said Rosemary. "I bet she's hiding out around there if she's managed to make it through the veil. We could go there tonight and camp out. See if we can find her."

"Sounds like a plan," said Dain. "Count us in. You might need fae backup."

"Sounds like an adventure," said Finnigan, with a grin.

"Okay," said Rosemary. "Meet there at eight."

"What will you do until then?" Dain asked.

"I suppose I'll go home and prepare," said Rosemary. "Maybe Athena will have some ideas. She's good at strategy."

"You might want to check on her," said Dain. "I just got a strange feeling that I can't quite explain."

Thirty-Five

Rosemary opened the door to her daughter's room and screamed.

A mysterious wind whipped around the room as Athena stood, suspended in mid-air, surrounded by her paintings which floated around her, suspended in a web of pink light.

"Athena!" Rosemary called out, squinting through the light at her teen, to see that Athena's eyes were blank. Not only that, they were glowing!

"Athena!" Rosemary tried again, but there was no response. She stepped cautiously into the room, worried that the spell, whatever it was, might attack her somehow. However, it just seemed to continue as it was as Rosemary approached her daughter. *It must be her own magic,* Rosemary reasoned, looking at how Athena's paintings appeared to be holographic, as they spun slowly around her. Athena, herself, still held a brush in one hand, glistening with paint. *She must have been painting when her magic kicked in and took over.*

She reached out for Athena's leg, trying to pull her down, but the girl wouldn't budge. In desperation, Rosemary texted everyone she could think of who might know how to help – Dain, Una, even Fleur.

It wasn't long before they had all arrived and assembled in Athena's room. Elise had come along with her mother, but hung back near the doorway.

"It's definitely her magic," said Dain. "Only...not just the fae side, the witching side as well. It's all coming together in a kind of chemical reaction. She's so powerful!"

"Stop sounding like a proud father," Rosemary admonished, "and help me get her down!"

Between the five of them, they surrounded Athena.

"What do we do?" Elise called out, the swirling magic blowing back her hair which had turned a dark violet in concern.

"She's lost in her own power," said Dain. "Completely over-whelmed. It happens sometimes with especially powerful fae."

"We need to soothe her," Una said knowingly. "She needs to know we're here, to connect back down to us and to the earth. Talk to her. Let her know we care."

"Athena, we love you," said Rosemary, taking the hand Una offered her as they formed a circle around the zoned-out floating teen trapped in the vortex of her own power.

"Yes, we're here for you," Elise added. "It's okay. We'll look after you."

They continued to talk to her, while each of them drew on

their magic as Una instructed, combining it together, with the intention of soothing her.

Many long moments passed before the pink light began to fade. The paintings toppled to the floor, followed by Athena, who was saved from a rough landing only by Dain's waiting arms.

He carried her, still unconscious, to her bed and lay her down to rest.

"This is going to take more than a bit of ointment to fix," said Una.

"Athena?" said Rosemary gently. "If you can hear me, try to come back, love. We're all here. We care about you."

Athena remained perfectly still. Rosemary put a hand to her daughter's forehead. "She's burning up."

"I'll get a cold flannel," said Fleur. Una followed her out of the room in search of herbal supplies.

Rosemary looked at Dain and then at Elise, whose expression was stricken.

"You can talk to her," said Rosemary. "If you like."

Elise knelt down by the bed. "I'm sorry," she whispered. "I'm sorry you had to deal with this alone. Please...please be okay."

She kissed Athena's cheek.

Rosemary noticed a single tear forming in Athena's left eye, before streaming down the side of her face.

"Stand back," said Dain, as Athena's body began to glow.

There was a tapping at the window. Rosemary ignored it, thinking it was just a poor confused bird, but it persisted, even as Athena glowed brighter.

"I'll get it," said Dain. He pulled back the curtain to reveal a fuzzy silver squirrel. "I think he wants to come in."

"No!" Rosemary said. But it was too late – Dain had opened the latch. The creature pushed the window open then scurried across the room, jumped onto Athena's bed, and nuzzled into the side of her neck.

"Dain!" said Rosemary, outraged. "Get that filthy rodent off our daughter!"

The squirrel glared at her as if it had understood, then it turned back to Athena and nibbled at her ear.

Athena's eyes fluttered open. "What happened?" she asked, looking from the odd furry creature to Elise to her parents and then to Una and Fleur who had just arrived back in the room.

"Your magic," said Dain. "It went haywire…We tried to help, but you were out cold."

"And then that weird little critter did something to wake you up," said Rosemary, eyeing the squirrel suspiciously. He was rubbing his hands together and preening.

The little black kitten, Serpentine, chose that moment to pad curiously into the room.

"Get it, kitty!" Rosemary urged. Serpentine jumped up onto the bed beside Athena and approached the squirrel.

The little cat slowly moved forwards, nudged noses with the squirrel, and then walked off, as if satisfied.

"Oh goodness," said Una. "I've never seen a squirrel familiar before!"

"Familiar?" Rosemary asked, astonished. "Aren't they supposed to be cats?"

"Often," said Una. "But not always. They can be any kind of creature, in theory."

"I have a familiar!" Athena cried joyfully, cuddling the squirrel.

"Careful," said Rosemary. "It might have diseases."

Athena laughed, the colour returning quickly to her chest. "You're a sweet little nugget, aren't you?" she cooed. "You don't have any nasty diseases."

"Nugget?" Elise asked.

"Yes," said Athena. "I think that's his name." She grinned and Rosemary couldn't help but return the smile.

The cat and squirrel chased each other around playfully in the living room of Thorn Manor while everyone else sipped Una's restorative tea blend.

Athena had quickly recovered and colour was flushing her cheeks in a healthy way. In fact, Rosemary was relieved to see her daughter was looking even more energised than usual.

"You're sure it's not Finnigan who's behind all this?" Athena asked her father.

Dain nodded. "I'm sure. He's been with me most of the time."

Athena shrugged reluctantly. "I'd like to believe that he really is turning over a new leaf, but it's hard to get my head around it."

"So who is behind it then?" Fleur asked.

"Maybe it *is* the countess, and some witch is helping her?" Rosemary suggested.

Una frowned. "I don't like the sound of that."

Rosemary's phone rang. "It's Tamsyn calling. I'd better answer this." She put down her tea cup. "Hello?"

"Rosemary, is this a good time?"

"As good as any, I suppose. It has been a very long day!"

"Well, I think you might want to hear this," Tamsyn said.

"What is it?"

"I tried a location spell again, but a different one this time, and Elowen helped me. The poor kid is exhausted now! The magic really takes it out of her, you know, but they say our speciality works best in partnership."

"Yes," said Rosemary. "Are you saying it worked?"

"I think so," said Tamsyn. "The spell was a simple one, but powerful. We burnt a piece of paper with our question to find the location of the trouble, and all the ashes drifted to one place on the map."

"Why didn't I think of trying something like that before?" said Rosemary. "The simplest solution is often the best."

"Yes, well you'll never guess where the ashes landed," said Tamsyn.

Rosemary looked around the room, "Actually, I think I have a pretty good idea."

The pieces of the puzzle were coming together in her mind. The Flarguans had had their memory tampered with in a way that reminded Rosemary of fae magic, and the countesses' calling card had been left at their mansion. Rosemary also recalled something Sherry had said to her recently about feeling odd, as if the veil was being affected somehow. Sherry had disappeared into the fae realm for an entire year as a child and was unusually sensitive regarding the veil. All this implied one particular location in Myrtlewood where the veil was the thinnest, so if this really was fae magic and the countess was involved, it made sense that whoever was helping her would be in and out of that area. The wheatfield where Burk had taken her on their second date where the first feather was discovered was only a few miles from where a couple of suspicious people were sighted around that same time.

"Finn's Creek." Tamsyn spoke the words at the same time as Rosemary.

Thirty-Six

Rosemary got out of the car at Finn's Creek and Athena
came around to stand beside her. It was close to dusk,
but she had checked the lunar calendar and knew the
moon was almost full again, so they wouldn't be completely in the
dark, plus they had torches and magical light sources if needed.

"I wish you'd agreed to stay at home," said Rosemary.

"Not a chance." Athena grinned. "Now that my magic has
settled down, I'm ready to get to the bottom of this."

Rosemary had tried to encourage her daughter to rest after
the shocking incident earlier. She herself thought she might be
better off staying at home too, only her spidey senses were
tingling. She could feel the energy building and she was sure this
was the place the trouble was all emanating from.

Dain, Fleur, Elise, and Una had insisted on coming too,
despite the possible danger.

Rosemary had messaged Burk as a backup, hoping the vampires might be able to lend some assistance as night fell. The night was approaching now after the longest day in history as far as Rosemary was concerned – move over Summer Solstice. Whoever made the normal rules for time clearly hadn't accounted for those days when one apprehends bigoted witches, gets magically arrested, and then finds one's daughter floating in mid-air in a terrifying magical trance.

"So what's the plan?" Una asked, approaching with Fleur behind her.

"We just kind of go in and scope it out, I suppose," said Rosemary. "But be careful. Here, I have supplies."

"My supplies," Athena corrected.

They were both carrying bags of Athena's various concoctions. They handed some of them around to their friends.

"Keep these in your pockets," said Athena. "Don't throw them unless you've got a clear target and you're prepared to make some noise."

"Or at least don't throw them at any of us," said Dain with a chuckle.

Finnigan was with him, standing slightly apart from the rest of the group. He looked uncomfortable and so did Elise, but Athena had a determined expression on her face.

"What is going on here is big and powerful," she said. "Powerful enough to cross to the other side of the world and sabotage the witching parliament."

Rosemary agreed. "Keep your eyes peeled for anything strange. The first stage is just to scope out the area in pairs. Fleur and Elise can pair up. I'll go with Athena, Dain with Finnigan... and I suppose Una can come with us too."

"What about me?" said a deep silky voice from behind Rosemary. She turned to see a rather handsome vampire in a suit. She ginned at Burk and embraced him.

"Get a room, Mum," said Athena. "I'm definitely not on your team now."

Rosemary narrowed her eyes. "Change of plans, then. If Athena doesn't want to go with me, I'll go with Burk. Una, you can partner up with Athena."

Dain looked somewhat taken aback and Rosemary realised he hadn't really been around them much since she and Burk started seeing each other.

"Just as well," said Athena making a slightly sick face. "I wouldn't want to be with you two lovebirds. It's disgusting."

Rosemary chortled.

"Alright," said Athena. "So we spread out carefully and then we'll come back together in fifteen minutes and share everything that we've seen. Then we'll make a plan based on having more information."

"Shouldn't the plan come first?" Dain asked.

Athena shook her head. "What's the point in making a plan when we don't have enough to go on?"

"Fair point," he said.

"So clever, isn't she?" Rosemary muttered, proudly patting Athena on the shoulder.

"Stop it, Mum," Athena grumbled, though she did shoot Rosemary a little smile.

248

"Alright, let's go," said Rosemary. She took Burk's hand and began making her way across the road towards Finn's Creek.

It had been a hot late summer day and the grass was brown and going to seed. The forest around them was dry. The creek itself was just a shy trickle without enough water for its usual rushing current. The willows looked like they were wilting even more than usual, but as they made their way further into the woods, the air was thick with magic.

"It's a little bit eerie," said Rosemary.

"You call this eerie?" said Burk. "You've been to my house."

Rosemary laughed. "Your family are not that bad. In fact they're kind of growing on me."

"You've only met them twice," said Burk. "They still have time to scare you off."

"Don't count on it," said Rosemary, pulling him close and giving him a quick kiss.

"As lovely as this is, don't we have other things we're supposed to be doing?" said Burk.

"Of course we do. Stop distracting me. Come on this way." She led him across the creek and through the woods, looking for signs of the countess.

As they wandered further, the magic became more visible. It almost looked like webs strung from the trees, and the air was soupy. It felt as if Rosemary had to wade through it. A soft violet glow lit the forest floor that reminded her distinctly of the fae realm, and orbs of purple light floated in the air dotted through the woods.

"This is very odd," said Rosemary. "Someone has definitely

been messing with the veil. Maybe that's why Sherry has been feeling off lately. She's sensitive to this stuff."

"Wait. I saw movement," said Burk.

Rosemary looked in the direction he was pointing and caught a glimpse of a figure in an elaborate dress disappearing through the trees.

They snuck closer.

Out of the corner of her eyes, Rosemary spotted movement in the bushes. On closer inspection she recognised familiar blue polyester. "What on earth?"

"Rosemary!" said Gerald's voice.

"Dad? Mum? What are you doing here?" Rosemary asked her parents. They looked dishevelled and their wrists were bound in green vines. "Are you alright?"

"We're been held here," said Mariana.

Rosemary gasped.

Gerald nodded. "Yes. By a very strange woman, ungodly and possibly evil. But she feeds us. We've been praying for her soul."

Rosemary struggled to free her parents as quickly as possible. "How long have you been here?"

"A day or two," said Mariana. "But we've lost track of time. She asked us a lot of questions about you, actually. But when it was clear we weren't giving anything away she got bored of us."

It was perplexing to Rosemary that the countess would kidnap her parents, of all people, but it showed she was desperate for information. Fortunately, Gerald and Mariana Thorn knew nothing, so while their plans to leave town had clearly been interrupted, at least they were safe and their capture hadn't been able to give the countess the upper hand.

Rosemary and Burk helped her parents in the direction of the parked cars. Rosemary was relieved they seemed to be fine. "Can I drive you to the police station?" she asked.

"No, no dear," said Gerald. "Really, we're fine."

Rosemary heard a noise up ahead. She held her finger to her lips. "Shh."

There was another sound, like branches breaking. "Here, take my car keys. I've got to sort something out," Rosemary whispered to her parents. She pointed them in the direction of the car.

She stepped forward, with Burk close behind.

A woman stepped out of from behind a dense clump of trees, dressed in a silver-and-black-striped silk gown.

"I don't believe it," Rosemary said, not bothering to keep her voice down. "Elamina!"

"What are you doing here?" Elamina asked with a sneer.

"Me?" said Rosemary. "I'm here to try and find the cause of all this political magical mayhem. I thought we were after Leithrein. But it turns out that you're here instead, in suspicious circumstances."

Rosemary glared.

"Leithrein?" Elamina gave a little laugh and Rosemary noticed that there were others behind her, various fancily dressed witches. She recognised some of them as being from Bermuda.

"Yes, the fae countess, Leithrein. Well, go ahead. Explain yourself," said Rosemary.

Elamina looked at her. "Really?" She furrowed her brow. "My poor, simple cousin. I know you don't like me very much, but it seems like you've been caught red handed."

"Excuse me?" said Rosemary.

Elamina shook her head sadly. "With your vampire friend here... Really, we should have kept a closer eye on you."

"What on earth are you talking about?" Rosemary asked. "I'm not sure what it is you're doing just now, or how you're channelling fae magic, or where you're getting all those purple feathers from but..."

Elamina chortled. "Me? You can't turn all your suspicious antics on me."

"Don't be ridiculous," said Rosemary. "You're the one who's suspicious. What are you even doing here?"

"Oh, Rosemary, stop making a fool of yourself. I don't need to explain myself to you. But if you must know..." Elamina paused and looked around. "We were having a perfectly lovely day of croquet and polo with cucumber sandwiches to go around, weren't we?" The crowd of snobby witches all nodded and murmured agreement. "We were just getting to the point of having a fabulous dinner when I sensed a sort of magical warning signal. I checked all the detection instruments in house and they were all giving off strange readings. Mamma and Pappa said we shouldn't bother. We should carry on having fun. But I was concerned, and so a group of us decided to investigate."

"And let me guess," said Rosemary. "Your magical implements brought you here?"

"Through a strong process of deduction, yes," said Elamina. "I could tell it was fae magic, you see, and I had a suspicion based on some other odd occurrences. This is where the veil is the thinnest in this area, you know."

"I do know that," said Rosemary. "I know very well, in fact."

She gave Burk a look. "I don't buy it. It's too much of a coincidence for you to be here. You must be working with *her*."

A sound of laughter emanated from behind Rosemary. She turned to see none other than Leithrein, the Countess of Western Eloria, tall and elegant in an elaborate dress of purple skeleton leaves and feathers. She was flanked by her fae guards, dressed in green leafy outfits.

"You humans are so amusing. To think that I'd stoop to work with one of you." She looked around at them and then narrowed her eyes at Rosemary. "You! You're the one who drugged me."

Elamina glared at her cousin.

"What?" said Rosemary. "It was only cream. You would have done the same in the circumstances."

"Rosemary," said Elamina though gritted teeth. "She's nobility. Show some respect."

The fae countess laughed again. "So funny, you little creatures," she said, though she was roughly human sized and shaped, herself.

"Erm, your...highness," said Elamina. "Given you're the one who has been causing all the trouble..." She turned back towards the other witching folk behind her. "I'm afraid we must detain her immediately."

Leithrein giggled. "So amusing to think that *you* could detain *me*," she said. "But if you must know, yes I may just be the one you seek. I don't want a treaty after all. It would somewhat sabotage my attempt at gaining power in the realm. You've all just been so self-absorbed you barely noticed."

"I can't believe this," said Rosemary. "You're just going to stand here and confess to everything? Well, go on then, show us how clever you are."

There was a gleam in Leithrein's eye. "It was easy to cancel your flights," she said to Rosemary. "Then forge the note saying you were no longer invited. But you managed to turn up in Bermuda anyway. You little minx." She laughed.

"And while you're in the middle of proudly confessing," said Rosemary, "you might as well make it clear that you killed that vampire girl Burk and I found in the field."

"A nice touch, wasn't it?" said the countess. "It was a warning. I was trying to get you to stay away. Only, as thick as you all are, you never listened."

"And you were the one who went to the Flarguan mansion and messed everything up. Why was that?" Rosemary asked.

"Silly girl. I followed you there, if you must know," said Leithrein. "After the Lughnasa ritual. I saw you sneak into their garden. So, of course I had to take a look. My curiosity got the better of me. Then upon investigating the inhabitants of the house, they called me awful names and I had to punish them."

Rosemary shrugged. "I guess I can sort of understand that one..." Burk raised his eyebrows. "Not that it's alright to go wrecking people's houses and tying them up or anything."

Rosemary had a thousand more questions, but the witches were approaching the countess.

"Stop," said Rosemary. "Don't underestimate her."

Leithrein gave them all a mischievous look. Then, with a flourish of her arm she and her guards disappeared.

"Follow them!" Elamina cried.

"Into thin air?" Rosemary asked incredulously.

Elamina shook her head, with a scathing expression. "It's just an enchantment. They haven't really teleported at all. Follow them through the woods. They're just hard to see."

Rosemary and Burk began to run in the direction that Leithrein had been standing in. Sure enough, leaves rustled. The grass was bent back as if footsteps were pushing it down, but moving fast.

They followed the subtle disturbances to a clearing.

"Stand back, you fools," said Leithrein, her invisibility slipping away.

She was holding a silver knife which seemed to glow in the moonlight. She raised it up and began cutting into the air.

A door started peeling back between the realms. "Bother," she said. "I still can't do it on my own. Fetch the halfling," she said to her guards and then turned a wary glare on Rosemary and Burk. "Don't even think about approaching." She held out her hands in front of her, creating a kind of green glowing forcefield in the air, surrounding her and the remaining guards.

Thirty-Seven

"What's going on?" Athena asked, reaching her mother's side. "Why is Elamina here with all those guys?"

Rosemary rolled her eyes and looked around for her cousin, who was nowhere in sight.

"She's not behind all this, is she?" Athena asked.

"I'm afraid not," said Rosemary. "As satisfying as that would be...It seems she just came to the same conclusion as we did that something weird was going down here – with the help of her magical instruments."

"I just saw her, back there. Why's she got all those servants with her and why are they carrying big trolleys?"

Rosemary shrugged. "Let's hope it's a big magical arsenal."

"Hey look," said Athena, as their other friends appeared in different spots around the clearing, all looking at the eerie green light.

"Ahh, here he is," said Leithrein.

"Oh no." Athena felt her gut tighten in shock as a familiar man in a green waistcoat entered the clearing, making his way towards the countess.

"That's him!" Rosemary hissed. "The travelling minstrel."

"Tell me something I don't know." Athena groaned.

"I knew he was a baddie," said Rosemary.

"You're right this time," Athena admitted.

"You were supposed to get him to leave town," Rosemary said to Burk.

"I did. But clearly that doesn't mean he stayed out of town."

"Look, he's helping her cut the doorway," said Athena.

Rosemary nodded. "She said she couldn't do it on her own. He must be like you."

Athena looked at the way Cailean was helping the fae countess to cut an enormous door through the veil.

"We've got to do something," she said, not bothering to keep her voice down as more fae guards began to emerge from the doorway. "Quick. We have to stop them somehow, before it's too late!"

"It was too late a long time ago," said Leithrein with a cackle, as many more guards stormed through.

"Oh no you don't," said Elise, throwing one of Athena's charms. It ricocheted off the green forcefield, sparking fires around the forest.

"No!" said Athena.

"I didn't know," Elise said regretfully.

Rosemary pulled some water out of the air to douse the fires.

"But how can we stop her if we can't get through the shield?" Athena asked.

"I'll take care of this," said Elamina, entering the circle. She held up her arms and closed her eyes. The green of the force-field suddenly burst into violent red flames. Energy flickered and then died out, leaving only ashes falling onto the forest floor.

"Attack!" cried the countess.

Dozens of guards who had already emerged through the door in the veil began to run towards them, and the battle began.

Athena kept an eye on Cailean. She used her magic to blast the guards away as they came at her. Thankfully, her powers came to her more easily than ever before, perhaps because she was so close to the veil, but also probably due to her fae powers coming in properly.

Her squirrel familiar poked its head out of her bag.

"You didn't bring him!?" Rosemary said from beside her.

"He wouldn't say no," Athena replied.

"Don't be ridiculous." Rosemary hurled a fireball at one of Leithrein's guards. "He can't talk."

"Really, he insisted," said Athena. "Now pay attention to what you're doing."

She sent her magic out in a ray of golden energy and hurled one of the guards into a tree.

"I'll take the countess," said Rosemary. "Or would you rather I handle the minstrel?"

"He's all mine," said Athena with an enraged gleam in her eye. She rounded on Cailean, who was leaning, nonchalant, against a nearby tree.

"There you are, my love," he said lazily, as Athena approached.

He pulled a ukulele out of his bag and started to tune it.

"No you bloody well won't!" said Athena. She blasted the instrument away as more guards came through the tear in the veil.

"Hit them with everything you've got!" Elamina yelled as she appeared in the clearing, flanked by servants and fancy Bermuda witches. They began to hurl not only the magic at the fae guards, but also a number of items from the trolleys they'd brought with them, that turned out to be laden with all kinds of fancy foods.

"Especially the cream cakes," Athena called out as gourmet canapes came flying through the air.

One landed on Cailean's nose. He looked unimpressed. "Not cream, I'm afraid. I've never been partial to the stuff, anyway. How about you, my dear? Surely if we are to be married it will pay for me to know your taste in d'oeuvres."

"It wasn't just my magic, was it?" said Athena. "You little rat. You put a spell on me."

He shrugged. "Your magic, my magic. What's the difference? We fit together, you and me. You might think it a passing fancy, but you know we are the same."

Athena glared at him. "The same doesn't necessarily make a good pairing. Besides, we couldn't be more different. You're a traitor."

He laughed. "A traitor? Hardly. I serve only myself."

"And the countess?"

"Well, she pays me handsomely for my brilliant skills. The beautiful thing is I don't even need an instrument when I have my voice." He opened his mouth and a musical note came forward, and resonated through around the crowd.

They all began to dance a little jig as the minstrel began to sing a fast Irish song.

"Oh no you don't," said Athena. Despite the amusing sight of the battle turning into a dance, she had to put a stop to it. She held out her hands and grabbed at the magic she could now see, pouring forth from Cailean's mouth.

She pulled it like a rope, one hand after another.

Cailean clutched his throat as Athena continued to pull the magic out of the air. It turned a sickly brown colour in her hands.

She wrinkled her nose but wasn't too surprised at the icky nature of his energy. Although, she was stunned at this new ability she seemed to possess.

She dragged the remnants of the magic from the minstrel. It globbed in her hands like sickly bile. Athena grimaced. "Now, what do I do with it?" she muttered to herself.

Cailean made a choking sound and fell to the ground.

"Give it back!" His voice was raspy. "That's mine!"

It dawned on Athena that she held more than fleeting power in her hands – as gross as it might be. She had managed to grab hold of the very essence of the minstrel's magic. But what to do with it?

A stone caught her eye and Athena bent down towards it, willing the magic to embed itself in the inert object.

The stone absorbed it like a sponge. It glowed for a moment and then went back to looking normal.

"What a relief." Athena used a scarf from inside her satchel to pick the stone up carefully. She put it in her bag.

"That was amazing," said Elise. "What are you going to do with it?"

Athena looked around at the carnage.

The guards were still fighting the witches off to one side, but dozens of vampires had appeared at the forest to join them in the battle against the fae. Burk must have phoned in reinforcements.

Rosemary was still locked in a magical battle with Leithrein.

Athena sighed and smiled at Elise. "Bury it, I guess. But we should probably help with this first!"

Thirty-Eight

Rosemary felt exhaustion creep in as she dodged another attack of green lightning from Leithrein. She looked around quickly to check that Athena was okay and take stock of the battle.

Dain had been darting through the crowd, punching the fae guards, confidently taking them down. Clearly he knew their weak spots. Rosemary caught a glimpse of him near the tear in the veil. He glanced around with a desperate expression and then flung his arms towards the gateway where fae soldiers were still emerging. A light shone out and Rosemary wondered whether he was trying to repair the veil, but a moment later he was swept back by another wave of uniformed fae coming through.

The Bermuda witches were hurling various enchantments around to little effect. They clearly hadn't had much experience fighting the fae.

The vampires were flinging fae around, left right and centre, somehow restraining themselves from feasting on their blood. Rosemary couldn't tell if that was a diplomatic move or just caution against devious fae enchantments. Either way, she was glad the fighting, as messy as it was, had not turned into a total bloodbath.

Rosemary hurled another ball of lightning towards the countess, who easily deflected it as if it was nothing more than a moth.

"You'll have to do better than that," she said as another wave of guards broke through from the fae realm.

Even with the vampires, they were outnumbered.

"I'm getting bored now," said Leithrein. She held up her hands and everyone froze.

Rosemary struggled, but she couldn't move. She looked around in panic.

The countess laughed and then clicked her fingers. Magical light pooled through from the fae realm, wrapping around all those present.

"Now that I've got you all here," she said, "what will I do with you? I know!" She had a gleam in her eye. "Perhaps I'll pop you into a marvellous little snow globe so I can shake you up and look at you from time to time."

She cackled.

Rosemary was badly wishing she'd remembered to invite the countess for a tea party before she lost the ability to move her mouth, though she wasn't sure if the law of the fae realm even applied on this side of the veil.

Panicking, she looked around for Athena.

She thought she could see her out of the corner of her eye,

standing there with Elise and Burk on the other side of the clearing.

They were all entangled now in Leithrein's powerful magic.

Rosemary had never felt anything like it. It was all over, she realised. The countess had always had the upper hand, she'd just been toying with them for her own amusement.

Her political manoeuvrings had been subtle over the past few weeks, but her power was far greater than Rosemary had realised and she must have been somehow connected to the Bermuda explosions, even if fae magic didn't work that way. Either that, or they had other powerful enemies they didn't know about yet.

Rosemary couldn't shake the feeling that they were all doomed.

She reached inside her for some kind of deep and powerful magic strong enough to break through the bonds, even to allow her to move...

Leithrein cackled again, but her laughter was interrupted by a tearing noise.

The gap in the veil beside them opened wider and a bright light like the sun poured through.

The countess's magic vanished and everyone began to move, looking around in confusion as they found themselves suddenly in what looked to be the light of day.

"Oh, no!" Rosemary looked to Burk, terrified he would fizzle into ashes.

He shook his head. "What is it?" he asked. "It's not the sun."

"Here comes trouble," said Dain.

A strange realisation dawned on Rosemary as a woman appeared, luminescent in the light.

"Queen Áine!" Leithrein cried. "Your majesty." She fell to her knees, as did all of the guards, bowing down before the monarch.

"What an utter disgrace," said the fae queen in an angelic voice. "It's time."

"Time for what?" Rosemary asked, squinting into the light. She could barely see any details in the brightness.

"Time I intervened," said Queen Áine.

Rosemary's eyes were adjusting to the light enough to see that the fae queen looked as if she was made from glowing sunlight. A lacy dress fluttered around her in many layers, and wings like butterflies floated two metres high at her back.

"Time for things to change," Queen Áine added.

"That sounds kind of good actually," said Rosemary.

The Arch Magistrate appeared with a pop, into the middle of the clearing, and looked around at the carnage.

"Miss Thorn," she said sternly, eyes locked on Rosemary. "I was notified of an unprecedented disturbance here and of course I find you! What in the name of the goddess is going on?" she asked, looking at the sprawled witches and fae guards. Then, catching sight of the fairy queen and the druid priestess, she bowed her head a little in respect.

"I'm afraid one of ours has been causing havoc," Queen Áine said. With a little wave of her hand, the fae countess floated into the air, spinning around gracelessly.

"It was all a terrible misunderstanding," Leithrein said.

"Are you telling me you weren't responsible for the chaos that has besieged us in Bermuda and here in Myrtlewood?" the Arch Magistrate asked, raising her eyebrows incredulously.

"Well, maybe some of it," Leithrein admitted. "But a treaty is a terrible idea. Even some of your witches agree."

"Be that as it may," said the Arch Magistrate. "A treaty would mean magical harmony such as we've not seen for hundreds of years."

She nodded at Burk's parents, who had emerged from beneath the pile of guards looking rather entertained.

"The vampires, the druids, the fae, and we ourselves as witches," the Arch Magistrate continued. "All of us here. We have the possibility of creating something of real value - a peace accord that will last for generations to come."

Queen Áine looked at her, blankly.

"Did you not receive the message your son sent?" the Arch Magistrate asked. She looked around for Dain.

Dain stuttered.

"My son?" said Áine. "You're here..?"

Her eyes landed on Dain and a reaction rang out like a tuning fork, sending shimmering light radiating around the clearing.

"After all this time..."

"I tried to send the message," Dain said as Athena came over to join her mother.

"Really?" Athena asked.

"I did. I got through the veil and everything. I sent a note with a pixie. It was too dangerous to risk trying to go all the way through West Eloria, what with her and her guards." He gestured to the countess.

"Daineathry," said the fae queen.

"Daineathry?" Athena hissed.

Rosemary giggled.

"My son, come closer," Queen Áine said, clearly shocked. Tears began to stream down her face. "You were so young, my beloved boy. You were so young when you left. Did somebody take you?"

"Not exactly, Mother," said Dain. "I mean, I was kidnapped by Leithrein, but that was a little bit later on. First, I ran away... just to tell you the truth."

"You were just a boy," Áine repeated as everyone watched on in hushed silence. "Tell me what happened."

"Err, long story short," Dain started, "I made it through the veil. I was sick of all the politics, you see, and I'm sorry."

"It was you who summoned me, was it not?"

Dain nodded. "I sent a distress signal through. We needed backup."

"We believed you were dead," said Queen Áine. "What has kept you away all this time?"

Dain looked towards Rosemary and Athena, clearly unable to find the words, but he didn't need to.

"I see," said the fae queen. "You were in love...and it seems I have a granddaughter."

Athena gulped.

Queen Áine looked between her and Dain for a moment and then waved him closer. He stepped forward and conversed with his mother. Rosemary and Athena looked at each other, unable to hear the conversation but clearly wondering what was being said. A few moments passed and then Dain stepped back, a serious expression on his face.

"Come here, child," said the fae queen, gesturing for Athena to step closer.

Athena hesitated and Rosemary felt a surge of anxiety. Queen Áine was clearly powerful and could be dangerous, but she didn't seem anything other than interested in meeting her surprise family member. Rosemary nudged her daughter and gave her an encouraging nod and then watched as Athena walked forward towards the golden glowing light.

Thirty-Nine

As Athena stepped forward, the light seem to wash right through her, making her feel calm, and tranquil.

"Grandmother?" she asked.

Despite the tranquillity, there was such power borne by Queen Áine that Athena trembled.

"Closer, child, so that I may see you."

"Athena stepped closer still, noticing that despite all the light pouring through, the fae queen had not crossed over into the earth realm. She stood in the doorway, her magic shining through.

Athena took another tentative step closer to the powerful magical fae queen. Áine reached forward, placing a finger on Athena's forehead. A radiant light shone out. It felt like molten gold moving through her.

For a moment, Athena felt like she was burning up on the inside. Like she was being judged and found worthy. Terror struck her heart at the possibility that she could be disapproved of or reviled or hated for being who she was, for having a human mother and a fae father, then she heard the sound of a lullaby.

"Calm your fears, child," said the fae queen. "You are indeed one of us."

Reassured, Athena smiled. Up close, the fae queen's light was almost too bright to look at. Athena blinked as she took in her grandmother's ageless face. "It's nice to meet you, finally," she said. "Despite the circumstances."

She looked around at the chaos.

"These are interesting times," said the fae queen. "I must leave, soon. It takes much of my power to be in this location between the realms."

"You can't come through," Athena said. It was a realisation rather than a question.

"I'm afraid I cannot cross through to your world."

"We could come visit you, I guess," Athena suggested. "As long as you promise it's not dangerous." She looked towards Dain. He shrugged.

"My son," Áine said, turning to Dain. "You must return to our world. Spend time with your family."

Dain hesitated.

"At least for a visit," Áine added.

Dain nodded. "I guess I can do that, Mamma. It was nice to see you."

Queen Áine dried her eyes. "It has been a day of losses and of great gains." Her voice rang out, although her light had begun to fade slightly. She raised her arms and all of the fae guards were swept up into the air into a large bubble and floated through the gap in the veil, which stretched even wider to let them all past the fae queen.

"I have lost a countess," said Queen Áine.

"No!" the Leithrein shrieked. "Please. Spare me! I will do anything...even grovel."

"You have tarnished the reputation of our entire Queendom and put many lives at risk."

"It was all a misunderstanding!" Leithrein wailed.

"Clearly, you came here to do harm," said the fae queen.

The Arch Magistrate cleared her throat. "And as the harm was done in this realm, *we* should have the right to exact punishment."

Leithrein sneered. "As if you pitiful witches have enough power to punish me."

The Arch Magistrate grimaced.

"You must be stripped of your title and powers," said Queen Áine.

Leithrein let out a low groan. "Anything but that!"

"And banished."

"Nooooo," Leithrein wailed. "I can't possibly live in this stupid, heavy place!"

"These are the consequences of your actions," Áine continued sadly. She held out her hand as if reaching into the air, and gave a little tug. Dark green energy flooded out of the former countess. Queen Áine seemed to absorb it, growing brighter once more. Leithrein hung limply in the air.

"Now I will leave you here, to face the consequences from the witches you so afflicted, stripped of your power."

"She's feeling generous," said Dain. "The mother I grew up with would show a lot less mercy."

"I have gained family," said the fae queen, and she smiled. "Now, I am sure the countess did not work alone. There are political issues to attend to in my realm. Someone powerful must be supporting her and there are urgent matters to address at court. I must go."

"But the treaty!" said the Arch Magistrate, clearly losing her cool.

Queen Áine regarded her coolly. "I have agreed to no such thing."

The Arch Magistrate paled and stuttered, but it was too late.

Radiant light burst forth once more before it faded and the hole in the veil sealed itself, leaving the forest looking almost normal again.

"Well, that was something," said Athena.

Forty

L eithrein writhed and groaned on the forest floor.
Rosemary couldn't help feeling a morbid satisfaction,
given all she'd put them through.

"I suppose that settles things," said Rosemary.

"I'm afraid not," said the Arch Magistrate.

Rosemary looked at her, a cold, creeping dread through her
veins. "Oh...no."

"What is yet to be resolved?" the Druid priestess asked.

"The countess did not act alone," said the Arch Magistrate.
"It wasn't fae magic which caused the explosion in Bermuda. It
was a witch."

A hush echoed around the clearing as the Arch Magistrate
raised her hand and pointed.

"Rosemary Thorn, your magical signature was identified at
the site of the blast, as you have previously been informed."

Athena looked at Rosemary. "Err...I was going to tell you,"

Rosemary whispered. "Apparently I'm under arrest or something."

She turned back to the magistrate. "It clearly wasn't me," said Rosemary. "I was just fighting her. Plus, the idea of peace sounds bloody good about now."

"It must be a mistake," said Athena.

"Yeah, can't two magical signatures be similar? Or maybe someone was forging mine?"

The Arch Magistrate shook her head. "The identification process is far superior to fingerprints and the like, that's why it takes some days to get the results back..."

"How dare you betray us," said Elamina's mother, with a scowl.

"Actually," said Elamina, stepping forward. "I sense foul play." To Rosemary's utter astonishment, her cousin stalked over to the fallen countess, ignoring her parent's protest.

"I believe my cousin is innocent," Elamina said. She stuck out a silver heel and stepped on Leithrein's wrist.

The disenfranchised fae screamed.

"Stop with the theatrics," said Elamina. "Tell us. What did you do?"

Leithrein cackled maniacally. "It was really quite clever," she gloated. "I simply disguised myself as a helpless old woman and asked a witch to assist me. Actually, the rest of you should be ashamed of yourselves." She looked around. "I asked several of you to no avail, until this one stopped to help me."

"Great," Rosemary grumbled, though she did feel a lightness in her chest as the lead weight of dread dissipated. "That's what I get for being a good magical citizen?"

Elamina looked at Rosemary scornfully.

"What?" Rosemary asked. "It seemed plausible to me!"

"Really, Mum?" said Athena.

There was a murmur of laughter around the crowd.

"Hey!" Rosemary said defensively. "At least I tried to help, not like you lot. Besides, how was I supposed to know?"

Forty-One

Rosemary and Athena arrived back at the house to find Marjie and Papa Jack busy in the kitchen.

"We hope you don't mind," said Marjie, hugging Athena and Rosemary in turn. "Una called me to tell me what happened and I thought you might be in need of some good old fashioned nourishment."

Rosemary smiled. "Of course I don't mind," she said. "As long as neither of you mind if we slink up to bed in exhaustion after we've had some dinner. What is it? It smells amazing."

"I'm just roasting some vegetables for my famous spiced pumpkin and sweet potato soup," said Marjie.

"Sounds perfect," Rosemary replied as Papa Jack handed her steaming mug of hot chocolate.

Though it was getting rather late in the evening, everyone had been too wired to rest. She had invited the friends who'd helped at Finn's Creek over for a chance to relax and decompress before they went home. Sherry and Liam had come too, bringing some supplies of mulled mead from the pub. Burk had been invited too, of course, along with his family who'd helped in their fight against the fae countess' guards, but they'd politely declined. Apparently some urgent vampire matters had come up that they'd had to attend to.

Rosemary made a slight detour on the way home to Thorn Manor but was pleased to see people had already gathered in the lounge. It was only ten-thirty, but it felt much later as they'd all been out since sunset.

"So it was the fae, after all," said Marjie. "I hope they didn't give you too much trouble."

"It's rather a long story," said Rosemary. "I might have to change my opinion on the fae."

"Why is that, then?" Marjie asked.

"Well, my grandmother showed up," said Athena. "And she turned out to be okay."

"Wonders never cease!" said Marjie. "The fae queen, herself, right here in Myrtlewood." She smiled. "I'm just glad you're both back safe and sound."

"My parents seemed particularly confused," said Rosemary. "Apparently the countess had kidnapped them and was keeping them as sort of pet hostages in the forest for a few days."

"Oh, no, that can't be good," said Papa Jack.

"Does that mean they know about magic now?" Marjie asked.

"I'm afraid so," said Rosemary. "I tried to send them to the car while we sorted out the magical mayhem, but apparently they couldn't resist sneaking a peak at what was going on. They're fine, just a little overwhelmed. We just dropped them off in town, at the inn, for some peace and quiet."

"I hope they don't go giving you any trouble," said Papa Jack. "I'll have to have words with them if they do."

"Hardly likely," said Athena, grinning. "At least for now, they think we're some kind of God-ordained superheroes."

"Well, it's not the worst possible interpretation," said Marjie. "At least they're not trying to exorcise you or anything."

"Exactly," said Rosemary. "I've had quite enough of that from them, and enough exercise too!" She took a long drink of the hot chocolate. "This has real cream in it, doesn't it?"

"Yes. Why is that dear?" Marjie asked.

"It's delicious, only Dain said he might stop by later to check on Athena," said Rosemary, getting comfortable by the window seat.

"I can make a little batch without it. How about that?"

"I'll help, Mrs Marjie," said little Zoya, enthusiastically.

"That's very sweet," said Athena. "I'm sure Dad would appreciate it. He does love Marjie's cooking."

Marjie grinned from ear to ear.

"No hot chocolate for me today," said Papa Jack as Marjie attempted to give him a refill. He had that sad and distant look in his eyes that Rosemary associated with great loss which he rarely spoke about.

"That's okay," said Athena. "More for me." She took a big gulp of the steaming beverage Marjie had just given her.

The doorbell rang and Rosemary answered it to find none other than the Arch Magistrate, herself.

"Miss Thorn," she said primly.

"It's just Rosemary. Am I in trouble again?"

The Arch Magistrate looked over her shoulder to where Reginald hovered, his eyes downcast, his top hat in his hands. "Hardly," she said. "I'm actually here to apologise. Isn't that right, Reginald?"

He nodded but didn't meet Rosemary's eyes. "It's seems there was a grave misunderstanding and we should not have accused you of the Bermuda...incident."

Rosemary cleared her throat. "Thank you for bothering to apologise in person, I guess. Would you like to come in for hot chocolate?"

Reginald looked up with a spark of excitement in his eyes.

"No," said the Arch Magistrate decisively. "I'm afraid we have other business to attend to tonight."

Reginald deflated somewhat.

Rosemary shrugged. "Suit yourself."

The Arch Magistrate nodded and, with a flick of her hand, Rosemary felt her wrist tingle. The silver bracelet she hardly recalled being there vanished.

"Interesting house," the Arch Magistrate muttered, looking up at Thorn Manor. "I don't think I've ever seen one before."

Rosemary's brow furrowed. "A house?"

"A living home," she explained. "They're very rare. Only the most powerful automancy families are said to have them. It's a treasure."

Rosemary smiled and patted the door frame. "Don't I know it!"

"Merry part," said the Arch Magistrate, issuing a rather old fashioned goodbye. "I would say until we meet again, though I'm hoping we won't find ourselves in quite this much chaos next time."

There was a slight smile twisting about her mouth and Rosemary couldn't help grinning. She said goodbye and returned to the living room to chat to Una and Fleur and fill Liam and Sherry in on the details of the unusual evening they'd just had.

Rosemary was just getting cosy as the smell of spiced chocolate wafted through the air when she heard the doorbell again. She rolled her eyes.

"I'll get it," said Athena, jumping up from the seat at the kitchen table. "It's probably Dad."

Moments later Rosemary heard Athena call out, "Mum! You might want to come here."

Rosemary made her way quickly to the door, concerned to hear surprise in her daughter's voice.

Dain was standing there with an apologetic smile on his face. He was flanked by two rather confused looking people dressed as if they'd been out exercising.

"You brought guests?" Rosemary said.

"Actually, I did," said Detective Neve, stepping forward. She frowned at Rosemary. "You should have told me you were going out to Finn's Creek earlier."

Rosemary shook her head. "No way. Not after last time I brought you into a dangerous situation. Nesta would kill me. Besides, you have a baby on the way."

Neve sighed. "Anyway, these are the people you keep asking me about."

"What?" said Rosemary.

"You remember, the couple who were found on the beach.

That's where I was all day. They woke up in the hospital, finally, and they don't believe me that they've been out for so long."

"Do you know where you live?" Rosemary asked the couple who had been standing there on the doorstep, looking dazed.

The two looked at each other and then turned back.

"What are your names?" Rosemary tried again.

"My name is Christina," said the woman. "And this is..."

Rosemary had been staring at the man's face. There was something familiar about it.

Neve cleared her throat. "I brought them here because they started asking about a few familiar names. You messaged about the gathering this evening and..."

"Do you remember what happened to you?" Rosemary asked curiously.

"Yes," said the woman. "We were going for a beach walk."

The man nodded. "That's right. We'd been visiting friends in Torquay and decided to find a nice spot along the coast for a stroll."

"Oh..." said Rosemary, and something began dawning in the back of her mind. She looked to Neve, who nodded meaningfully.

Just then, little Zoya skipped into view. "Mama?" She stopped, staring at the couple.

"Zoya!" They both cried at once.

"But how? Why is our daughter at your house?" said the man.

"We've always heard rumours of sirens taking people," said Neve. "We may never know why, or what happened to you all that time, but it seems you went for a walk on the beach three years ago and were taken."

"Don't be daft," said the woman. "This is some kind of practical joke, is it?"

"A reality show, maybe?" the man suggested.

"Papa Jack!" Rosemary called. "You're going to want to come here."

"Now, now, what is it?" Papa Jack said in his rich warm voice as he walked towards the doorway. His jaw dropped open and his eyes bulged in shock.

"I don't believe it!" he said finally. "Arjun?"

"Hey, Dad," said Arjun. "What are you doing here?"

Papa Jack, with tears in his eyes, ran to his son, wrapping him in a huge hug, and pulled his daughter-in-law in too. Zoya joined, of course. The couple remained confused for some time. They simply could not believe that the walk they felt they'd only just taken, perhaps the day before at most, had lasted three years and that they'd been kept alive under the sea for most of that time.

"Do you suppose it was a kind of peace offering?" Athena asked quietly, watching as the newly reconnected family caught up.

Rosemary shrugged. "You mean the sirens decided to return some people they'd taken from around here in the hopes that the witches would be less likely to retaliate? Could be."

"Maybe they even knew about the connection to us," said Athena. "Though that seems unlikely. Who knows, with magic?"

"I'm so happy for Papa Jack," said Rosemary, tears stubbornly pushing their way out of her eyes. "He's such a lovely man and he deserves to have his family back."

"They didn't forget," Athena said. "Not like that woman you found on the beach."

"No," said Rosemary. "Maybe not everyone does. I know I never would have forgotten you."

Athena smiled at her. "I would be distinctly unimpressed if you did."

"Exactly," said Rosemary. "I'd never live it down."

Forty-Two

"Wow, that was some day," said Elise, joining Athena as she sat in the living room after their late supper. "I hope it's not weird that I'm here. Mum wanted to come and wind down a little bit before we go home and I thought it might be nice."

"It's not really weird," said Athena. "But I do feel like..."

"I know," Elise said. "We haven't really properly talked."

Athena nodded. "Now it's probably not the right time either."

"You must be exhausted, I know."

"I am."

"I suppose there'll be plenty of time, in future," said Elise. She looked at Athena quizzically.

"What is it?" Athena asked.

"That stone, the one you sent the minstrel's magic into. What did you do with it?"

"I think it's still in my bag," said Athena.

"Want me to help you bury it?"

Athena smiled. "I suppose. Better sooner than later."

Athena picked up her bag and they wandered out to the back garden.

"Where, do you think?" Elise asked, carrying a spade that she'd found by the back door.

"Maybe off to the side?" said Athena. "I know you're supposed to bury weird magical things in the ground so that the energy can be returned to the earth, but I don't want any of it leaking out, so not anywhere we're likely to walk. Maybe over here,"

she said leading Elise to a spot at the very edge of the lawn.

"You don't want to put it in the forest?" Elise asked.

"No. I'd prefer to keep an eye on it just in case anything weird happens."

Elise pushed down the spade, tapping the ground. "Here?"

Athena nodded and watched as Elise began to dig.

"You know, I've been thinking," said Elise, and sudden dread struck Athena. Either Elise wanted to get back together, or she wanted to make the breakup more permanent. And though she still held Elise dearly in her heart, Athena didn't know how she could possibly deal with either situation. Everything had already been so troubling and overwhelming.

As much as she wanted to be with Elise, she felt like the time wasn't quite right. She still had so much to figure out, but it was obvious Elise needed to get something off her chest and Athena didn't want to die of curiosity over which way the wind was blowing.

"What is it?"

Elise looked at her. "You might not want to hear this," she said. "But I don't think I'm really ready to have a proper relationship."

Athena laughed.

Elise's eyes widened. "Not the reaction I was expecting."

"Sorry," said Athena.

"Care to explain your reaction?" Elise said, raising her eyebrow.

"Well, just then, I was dreading that you were either going to break up with me properly and, you know, in a permanent way, which would be awful."

"I'm not ready to do that, either," said Elise. "I know you've been through a tough time and I feel terrible for pushing you away like I did. It's just that..."

"Let me finish," said Athena. "I was also dreading that you're wanting to get back together."

"Really?" Elise asked. "Did I do something wrong?"

"No, it's just that I don't think I'm ready for a relationship yet either. Everything in my life has just been so chaotic. And I feel like there's all this expectation on me – regarding both sides of my family. I still...I love you.."

"I love you too," said Elise, a little sadly. "That's why it's so hard. I just don't know how to cope with everything. Life has been such a roller coaster and my insecurities get out of whack."

"Exactly," said Athena. "Err, I think you can stop digging now."

The hole was getting rather deep. Elise smiled at her. "Now what?"

Athena lifted her bag and withdrew the scarf-covered rock. "Okay, so just put it in the ground, I guess." She placed the rock into the hole. They both watched with some trepidation for a moment. When nothing happened Elise held up the spade and Athena gave a nod. She kicked some of the dirt back into the hole while Elise shovelled with the spade.

"You know," said Athena. "I do feel sad about things not working out between us."

"It is a little sad isn't it? But no matter what happens, I don't want to lose you, whether we're friends or girlfriends or whatever we are."

Athena smiled. "I don't want to lose you, either, whatever we are to each other."

"Maybe we can just be friends for now," said Elise. She finished filling the hole carefully, tapping down the dirt on top.

"Do we just leave it like that?" Elise asked.

"Yes," said Athena. "Apparently...that's what I've read, anyway. It's not worth risking adding any other magic to it in case it mixes and goes strange. The earth is the best medicine, she knows how to convert energy into whatever she needs."

"That's beautiful. Well, I suppose I'll be going home soon."

"I hope it's not awkward..." said Athena.

"What is it?"

"Friends are allowed to hug, aren't they?"

"Of course, they are."

Athena and Elise wrapped each other in a warm hug and Athena allowed herself to experience the feelings of love and loss, of acceptance and letting go. She also felt the glimmer of hope of future possibilities.

"It's not permanent," said Elise stepping back from Athena.

"What are you talking about?" Athena asked as they walked back towards the house.

"Whatever this is," Elise said. "I mean. It feels like it could change at any moment."

Athena smiled. "Who knows? Maybe one day we'll be ready to get back together again. But for now, we've always got each other's backs."

"Always."

Forty-Three

"This turned out to be a very good idea," Rosemary said, taking a sip of her mojito as she lounged by the pool in the emerald green hammock Athena had bought for her – as promised – at the local market that morning.

"I told you so," said Athena, casually swimming over as she completed another slow lap. "We definitely needed a holiday after all that, though Spain is a little closer than Bermuda."

"What a rollercoaster," said Rosemary. "It feels like we just skip from one big jumble of magical mayhem to the next."

"It certainly keeps life interesting." She floated on her back in the pool for a few moments while Rosemary savoured another sip of her tangy refreshing cocktail.

"So your parents," said Athena, returning to an upright position. "Do you think everything's going to be alright with them? They don't need counselling after being kidnapped by a mad fae aristocrat or anything?"

"They seem chipper," said Rosemary. "I gave them a quick call to check up on them before we left. Apparently, they're still convinced the countess was a demon and that we are doing God's work."

"Long may that strange misconception last," said Athena. "I was worried they'd start a witch hunt."

"There's still time," said Rosemary, with an ironic laugh.

"It's funny, isn't it?" said Athena. "The countess was leaving her calling card the whole time, but we kept thinking that was too obvious, that it couldn't possibly be her."

"Former countess," said Rosemary. "But yes. I think it was the explosion thing that most threw me off the scent. Dain was adamant fae couldn't create it."

"It's even funnier how the culprit turned out to be you!" said Athena with a laugh.

"Hilarious," said Rosemary, her voice dripping with sarcasm.

Athena had stopped laughing and was looking longingly into the distance.

"Sorry about things with Elise," said Rosemary.

Athena shrugged. "It's okay. Just never bring up that *musician* again."

"I'll do my best," said Rosemary.

"Do you really think a treaty is on the cards?" Athena asked.

"We'll see," Rosemary replied. "I suppose it depends on all parties coming to some agreement, including your queenly grandmother."

Athena sighed. "She's amazing! Almost like a goddess..."

"Don't get rose tinted glasses or anything," said Rosemary. "Remember, even gods and goddesses aren't perfect."

"I know that." Athena said as she got out of the pool and wrapped a towel around her. "This summer has seemed to last forever. I can't believe school starts back next week."

Rosemary smiled. "I'm glad they've got the proper campus up to standard again. It wasn't the worst thing, hosting everyone at Thorn Manor, but it will be less for me to worry about."

"Hey. It's almost eight o'clock," said Athena, checking her phone. "Don't you have somewhere to be?"

"I don't want to leave you all alone," Rosemary replied.

"Oh, go on. Have fun. I'll just be in the suite, reading."

Minutes later Rosemary walked out to the marina to see a handsome man, dressed in a white Spanish shirt and jeans. "I can't believe you came all the way over here for a date."

Burk smiled. "I wouldn't miss it for the world," he said, leading her onto a luxury sailing yacht.

"Of course, you have a boat," said Rosemary. "Can you make cheese, too? Because that would make you the perfect man."

"My culinary skills are usually reserved for dinners," said Burk.

"Pity..." Rosemary teased.

"I could learn," said Burk, leaning in close for a kiss.

"I think I could get used to this," said Rosemary, moments later, as she watched the water slip away around them, as the land faded from view to reveal more and more beautiful horizon.

"Boating?" Burk asked, adjusting a rope that Rosemary had previously assumed was just for show.

"No," said Rosemary. "This." She reached for his hand. "Dare I say...relationship."

"The R word, Miss Thorn," said Burk. "Now that, I wasn't expecting."

Rosemary's heart fluttered. She felt giddy, terrified. "It's funny how I can fight all manner of magical enemy and yet this... this scares me more."

"There's no pressure," said Burk.

"Exactly," said Rosemary. "*I* want this...which is even scarier."

"Let me see if I can help you take the edge off," said Burk, pulling her into a brain-melting kiss.

They jolted apart by a sound similar to a record being scratched.

"What the..."

Everything around them looked normal – the ocean lapping at the boat, horizon on all sides. Rosemary looked up to see a tear in the air. Little blue hands reached through, followed by arms and legs.

Burk furrowed his brow.

"What are they?" Rosemary asked, as dozens of small winged creatures with blue skin, wearing tiny kilts, burst into the air and gnashed their teeth at her. "And what do we do?"

"I think you'll find they're pixies," said Burk. "And in answer to what we should do...take cover and find the nearest usable weapon."

Epilogue

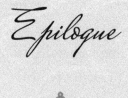

The path around her glowed a gentle violet as she walked along. Deep toned toadstools were dotted here and there, emitting their own light, surrounded by ferns and palms.

She walked more briskly than she usually did, towards her sacred space, letting her golden gown fall to the ground as she neared the pool.

In only her slip, Áine stepped into the tepid water, allowing it to soothe her as it always did. She submerged herself and floated there, suspended.

The journey had taxed her more than she'd ever admit, even to her closest confidants. To be a royal fae was to exude strength, especially for the queen. However here, at her pool, she could merely be as she was.

She stared up at the enchanted stars above her and then

allowed her eyes to close, just gently. Yes, the journey had been taxing, but it was also so much more!

She'd used a lot of power to cross the realm so quickly, but of course she had to answer the distress call. She could tell it was one of her family summoning her, and all those years he'd been gone she had held out hope of Dain's return.

It brought joy – so much joy – to see him again. Her lost son. Her little prince.

Her heart felt warmer and happier than it had in many years.

It wasn't only her son that she'd gained back that evening, there was his daughter too. A granddaughter!

Áine's heart sung at the thought.

Human on her mother's side, but powerful. Athena would do wonders in the fae realm. It might be a challenge, but Áine was sure it would be a perfect use of her energies. *Athena and Dain must come to the fae realm. They are part of our family, and are entitled to be with me, at court. They must be here, where they belong, and I must find a way to bring them home.*

Permanently.

Order Myrtlewood Mysteries book six!

A NOTE FROM THE AUTHOR

Thank you so much for reading this book! It was so much fun writing it. I love Myrtlewood with all its quirky characters and cozy magical atmosphere.

If you have a moment, please leave a review or even just a star rating. This helps new readers to know what kind of book they're getting themselves into, and hopefully builds some trust that it's worth reading!

You can also join the Myrtlewood coven - my reader list or follow me on social media. Links are on the next page.

About the Author

Iris Beaglehole

Iris Beaglehole is many peculiar things, a writer, researcher, analyst, druid, witch, parent, and would-be astrologer. She loves tea, cats, herbs, and writing quirky characters.

facebook.com/IrisBeaglehole

twitter.com/IrisBeaglehole

instagram.com/irisbeaglehole

Lightning Source UK Ltd.
Milton Keynes UK
UKHW010615270123
416054UK00001B/58